In the Dwellings of the Wilderness

The Literary Vampire Series

C. Bryson Taylor

"There are more things in heaven and earth, Horatio,
Than are dreamt of in our philosophy."
—*Hamlet* I. v.

DEAD LETTER PRESS
NEW KENT, VA

The Literary Vampire Series, Volume II:
IN THE DWELLINGS OF THE WILDERNESS
First published 2007 by DEAD LETTER PRESS

This edition © 2015

Cover illustration © Allen Koszowski 2015
"The Tomb of Obscurity" © Tom English 2015

Printed in the United States of America

ISBN-10: 0979633591
ISBN-13: 978-0979633591

SECOND EDITION
JULY 2015

DEAD LETTER PRESS
WWW.DEADLETTERPRESS.COM

CONTENTS

The Tomb of Obscurity

UNEARTHING A COPY of the first and, until now, only edition of *In the Dwellings of the Wilderness* is nearly impossible today. Like the ancient ruins depicted in the 1904 novel, the book was covered over by the sands of time: "...Dead and buried, waiting for us ... to lay it open to the light once more." Indeed, so obscure did it become that barely forty years after the weird novel's publication, E. F. Bleiler failed to uncover it while compiling his 1948 *Checklist of Fantastic Literature*.

Trying to dig up information on the novel's author is nearly as challenging. Sifting through contemporary fiction magazines, specifically *All-Story* and *Everybody's Magazine*, and bibliographic records, turns up only a few pieces of the literary puzzle. For instance, the author was born in 1880, and is credited with scarcely a handful of short stories and two novels, *In the Dwellings of the Wilderness* being the first, *Nicanor, Teller of Tales* (a story of Roman Britain) following in 1906. None of which exactly yields a complete or even mildly satisfying account of the author's life.

But sometimes providence smiles upon the literary archaeologist. Chancing upon the following inscription in the May 1905 issue of *The Writer* was most illuminating, and is recorded here in its entirety:

C. Bryson Taylor, whose story, "The Proof of Man," was printed in the *Cosmopolitan* for April, is a Washingtonian, and has been engaged in magazine and journalistic work for the past eight years. Her first story appeared in the *Overland Monthly* in 1898, but she says that *Everybody's Magazine* gave her practically her first start by running her serial, "The Wooing of Ah-té." *Everybody's* has also printed many of her short stories, articles, and sketches. Her first book, "In the Dwellings of the Wilderness," was published by Henry Holt & Co., and she has now a second book nearly completed, which will be much longer than her first, and wholly different in style and treatment. In response to many inquiries, Miss Taylor wishes to say that the quotation from which the title "Proof of Man" is drawn is taken from Franklin's "Poor Richard's Almanac": "The proof of gold is fire; the proof of a woman, gold; the proof of a man, a woman." (*The Writer: A Monthly Magazine for Literary Workers*, Volume XVII, January 1904 - December 1905; Boston: The Writer Publishing Company, 1906.)

So the author of the manly adventure *In the Dwellings of the Wilderness* was a young woman. She was probably about twenty-three years old when she wrote her strange tale of vampirism and Egyptology. Chances are, she had never visited an archaeological dig, or traveled to the Middle East, or anywhere outside of the country, for that matter. Notwithstanding, owing to her ability to evoke through her prose both the landscape and the mood of the desert world, Taylor easily transports the reader to the land of "the inscrutable East, brooding and somber, wise with forgotten evil lore."

In the Dwellings of the Wilderness appeared one year after the publication of Bram Stoker's *The Jewel of Seven Stars*, a dark fantasy which enjoys the distinction of being the first to deal with the resurrection of an ancient Egyptian mummy (and a *female* mummy, no less!). In light of this, L. W. Currey suggested that Bryson's novel might have been a deliberate attempt to combine themes from *The Jewel of Seven Stars* and Stoker's 1897 quintessential vampire novel *Dracula*.

Whatever its conceptual origins, *In the Dwellings of the Wilderness* remains an intriguing and well executed weird tale, one certainly worth being freed from the tomb of obscurity—and given another life.

Tom English
New Kent, VA

Tom English is an environmental chemist who enjoys writing weird stuff. His stories have appeared in several print anthologies including Challenger Unbound *(KnightWatch Press, 2015),* Gaslight Arcanum: Uncanny Tales of Sherlock Holmes *(Edge SF and Fantasy) and* Dead Souls *(Morrigan Books). Tom also edited the mammoth* Bound for Evil: Curious Tales of Books Gone Bad, *a 2008 Shirley Jackson Award finalist for best anthology. He resides with his wife, Wilma, surrounded by books and beasts, deep in the woods of New Kent, Virginia.*

In the Dwellings
of the Wilderness

CHAPTER I

In the Dark Backward and Abysm of Time

DEANE CAME OUT of his tent, lighting a particularly
unclean briar, and strolled over to where Merritt lay flat
on his back, his hands behind his head, staring out
over the desert into the painted sunset sky. Off to the
right were the excavations, gaping like raw wounds in
the monotone of brown desert sand; huge mounds of
out-flung earth, monstrous and grotesque, deep pits
and chasms with sloping ridges and embankments; in
the great mound called by the Arabs the Mound of the
Lost City, which overtopped and dominated all the rest,
wide trenches, long and deep, cutting far into the
hidden heart of it, by which men had ascended from
and descended to what lay below. To the left were the
small army of labourers, camped behind one of the
smaller untapped mounds, intent upon their meagre
supper of parched corn. The bluish smoke of a fire rose

from behind a jutting breastwork of earth where Ibraheem, the overseer, was making the thick, fragrant coffee of his land. Already the loneliness of coming night was upon the earth; already the sun had dipped below the desert's rim, and the fierce colour of the sky was fading. Away to the east, behind the camps, far to the edge of the world, the shadow of darkness was racing with swift, silent strides.

Deane sat down beside Merritt's prostrate figure. He was tall, and deep-chested, and thin-flanked, with a certain gravity about him which made him appear older than his years. His eyes were brown and quiet, his hair a brownish red, remarkably stiff and wiry; about his mouth were faint lines of humour. Merritt, short and thin and tough as whit-leather, grey of hair and keen of face, moved a hand from beneath his head, tilted back the hat that hid his face, and looked up at Deane.

"Where's Holloway?" he inquired.

"He took his camera early this afternoon and said he was going to get some views of what we've uncovered of the North Temple," Deane replied. "Seems to me we ought to find more tablets in there somewhere—well-preserved ones. This place is modern compared with some of the sites of other cities we've come across."

He eyed the excavations with interest, eager to probe the depths of their ancient mystery. Also he wished that Holloway would return. Holloway was young and ardently imaginative, and one could talk to him about the spell of fascination which this mighty grave held for one, the thoughts of greatness risen and passed away and lost which it conjured up. One could not easily talk to Merritt thus, because Merritt was an old hand at the business, eminently practical and hard as rocks, and matter-of-fact to his finger-ends, apt to confuse sentiment with sentimentality and consequently despise it.

6

The sun sank below the horizon and swiftly the world grew dark. From the men's camp came a mournful chant, subdued, and heard as from far away, and the measured thump of a drum. At intervals a donkey raised his voice, after the manner of a saw shrieking its way through wood. With the darkness came the stars, leaping into the black arch of heaven, great and of a number beyond all counting; the night-wind turned the heat of the day to sudden coolness, sweeping softly among the ruins. The mounds of earth, softened in outline by the darkness, loomed vast and shadow-like, melting into the sombre mystery of the night. Mingled with the chant of the natives and the occasional hee-haw of the donkeys was the fretful bleating of goats, destined for the masters' food. Around the jutting earthwork a faint gleam of light shone from the overseer's fire. Over all the night brooded, swallowing sound and motion in its immensity.

"Those brutes would work like cattle all day and sing like bullfrogs all night," Merritt said suddenly. He heaved himself on an elbow and shouted for Ibraheem. Soon this one came stalking from his fire, a blot against the night.

"Why are the men so noisy to-night?" Merritt wished to know.

"Ney pray for well-luck, saar," Ibraheem said, answering Merritt's Arabic with proud English, fluent and execrable, and an accent all his own. "Nis defunct citee is not good to be disturbed. Lord-God, He curse it in way back sometimes, and ne men are grief-ful and fearing of—um—ghos'. Ghos', yaas. Vurry ignorunt men."

"Oh, that's it, is it?" Merritt, losing interest, settled again to the ground. "Well, tell them they need not be afraid of ghosts. The last one died of old age a good thousand years ago."

"Vurry good, saar!" Ibraheem said, conceiving this the most correct and English response to make. Merritt and his men were the first Americans he had met, otherwise he would have said "All right." He fell back into the shadows; and by degrees the chant died to a whimper and a whine, and ceased.

"We'll get to the east wing of the palace to-morrow, don't you think?" Deane inquired.

Merritt stretched comfortably on the warm ground and cast his hat aside.

"I should think so." His voice became slow, hushed to accord with the quiet of the night. "The palace where those old people lived and died two thousand years ago. Fancy what this place must have looked like then, the centre and heart of a civilisation that throbbed with pulses as keen as ours. Tell you what, Deane, it gives me a queer feeling at the roots of my hair every time I come to a closed door or open a buried tomb. *'Think of it, old man; take it home to you and live on it! Yours is the first foot to cross that threshold, the first hand to pick up tablet or jar or potsherd since those old folks left it.'* That's what I say to myself every time. They died, or were killed off somehow, and they left their city behind them, deserted." Merritt's voice grew slower, with long pauses between his sentences. He seemed not talking to Deane at all. "Then the courtyards began to fill with dust and sand, just a thin layer at first, you know, with all the colours good and bright, and the walls standing. Then weeds began to grow between the stones, and the gardens went to jungle and the layer of dust deepened. By and by a wall fell ... out here in the loneliness, a dead city left to its fate.... Wild beasts made the halls their lair, and monkeys chattered in this very palace we are going to see to-morrow, and lizards slept on the steps in the sun.... And more walls fell, and the sand crept up around them, and there was never a voice to break the stillness, nor a sound except the dropping of a stone. Then by degrees the face of the world changed, and the earth, like an ocean wave, rose until the city was covered, and there were only misshapen mounds to show that life had been there. And the city was dead and buried, waiting for us, just us three from the other end of the world, to lay it open to the light once more."

Abruptly his voice ceased. In the darkness neither could see the other's face. Deane sat and listened silently, immeasurably surprised. Merritt the hardheaded, Merritt the practical, who would sneer at sentimentality, to rhapsodise thus? Deane knew that it is precisely the man most reserved and self-contained, who, when he speaks at all, will go to greater lengths even than the habitually confiding, and lay bare the deep, shy heart of him to its very roots. Deane also knew that when this rare mood fastens on such an one it is to be marvelled at and its tale held sacred; for always it will mark some crisis in the man's life, the outward sign of a stress which perhaps none but himself may know. And because Deane's every nerve thrilled in response to the suggestion in Merritt's words, and because that might be said in darkness, between men, which daylight would show up pitilessly and render commonplace and futilely inane, Deane said slowly, staring up at the great stars that blazed above them:

"I didn't know *you* felt like that about it too."

Merritt countered with quick eagerness.

"Do you? Can you put yourself back in that old vanished life when you come upon the broken corpse of it here, and reverence it? Can you build these ruined walls again, and see, instead of mounds and trenches, a city with tower-capped walls, and groves of trees, and gardens, teeming with human life whose very ashes have dissolved? That's what I do, every time. It began when I was a little shaver, back home. They wanted to make an engineer of me, but I said I'd rather dig up things that other people had built than spend my time building things for other people to dig up. It sort of took a grip on me—and it never let go."

Deane nodded sympathetically in the darkness.

"I know what you mean, all right. But—well, I had no idea that you felt—er—this way about it."

Merritt laughed.

"I don't know what made it all ooze out to-night," he confessed. "But I've been thinking about it a lot. It'll be a big thing, Deane. It will mean a good deal to all of us, if we can put it through."

"Why shouldn't we put it through?" Deane questioned.

Merritt sat up and felt himself for matches.

"I don't know!" he answered somewhat dubiously. "No reason, I suppose. But somehow, all along, I haven't been able to see us getting to the end of it. I can plan out to a certain point with a reasonable certainty, barring accidents and the will of God, that things will fall out as I intended. But beyond that point, in a way it is as though I had an inkling that it was the unexpected which would happen. Of course, it is merely nonsense. By the way, hasn't Holloway got back yet?"

"I presume so," Deane answered. "His boy left those rolls of films he insisted on bringing, in the sun yesterday, and they've melted. I told him films would be a good deal of a nuisance in a climate like this."

"He'll come out all right, I guess," Merritt said easily. "It's his first trip, and he's green, but he's a forehanded youngster, and he surely knows how to get good pictures."

The two fell into silence, conscious subtly of a new sympathy between them. Each had penetrated the other's shell, had touched the hidden spring of a feeling which both shared; and without more words it became a bond between them. They smoked quietly, at peace with themselves, with each other, with all the world.

A black figure grew out of the night and came over to them, with the faint glow of a cigarette stabbing a hole in the darkness.

"Apparatus all right?" Deane asked. "Get any views this afternoon?"

"Yes," Holloway answered. "I've been prowling. This place is great. Awfully lonesome sort of feeling it gives a fellow, though, to look into the holes we've dug and think what the old chaps would say if they could see us." Deane and Merritt, unseen, grinned in sympathy. "That brute of a boy got all my films sunstruck—four dozen rolls. I didn't expect to use them much, but I hate to have 'em go, on principle. I believe I'll turn in. Goodnight, everybody."

"'Night!" they chorused solemnly.

Holloway disappeared. Soon Deane followed him, and Merritt was left sitting alone in the night, with his hard, weatherworn face and his dream-woven fancies.

CHAPTER II

THE DOOR WHICH WAS CALLED FORBIDDEN

Before dawn the men had breakfast, and began work when there was light enough to see their tools. Holloway, trailing his tripod behind him, and followed by a boy with a case of plates, went from spot to spot, taking views. He was a cheery youth, lithe and active, with amazingly light hair, a pair of humourous blue eyes, a square-jawed face burned to a consistent and apoplectic scarlet, and hands much stained by chemicals.

Merritt, his helmet jammed well over his eyes, climbed up and down the trenches tirelessly, a wad of crumpled plans in hand. He was in all places at once, keen, clear-eyed, practical, overseeing and directing, called upon for help and advice in all directions. The mood of the night had come and gone; again he was as the world knew him. The labourers swarmed over and around the mounds like busy ants. At one side of a hill of earth and rubbish a file ascended the steep steps of trampled earth which ran down into the trenches, unending, ceaseless, bearing baskets of dirt. At the other side, down more steps, a file descended with empty baskets; from the bottom came the thud of pick and spade and the hoarse shouts of the foremen of the gangs. Above them was the clear morning sky, not yet heated to molten brass; around them the desert, vast and soundless; beneath them the fragments of an olden world, whose story was lost in the dimness of bygone ages.

Ibraheem climbed agilely to the top of the trench which had been opened farthest into the mound, spied Deane making cabalistic signs in a notebook, using one knee as desk, and hurried over.

"Saar," he announced, swelling with importance and the pride of his discovery, "the mens find a wall, unruinated, with a door and a writing upon it. Where are Mister Merritt?"

"By the temple wall, with Mr. Holloway," Deane answered. "Go call him quick."

Ibraheem went, at a dignified dog-trot; and Deane stuffed his notes into a pocket and ran down the trench to where the workmen, chattering shrilly, were gathered around a mass of débris. It was not the first find of the expedition, but each fresh discovery sent the same tingle of excitement through the entire outfit. For there is nothing more stirring than to stand at the threshold of a long-dead world, on the verge of entering, knowing that the next blow of the pick, the next step forward, may reveal either lost secrets of dead peoples which will shed fresh light through the grey mists of ages—or nothing; may turn a new page in the sealed Book of the Things that Were, or disclose a blank. Even the basket-men swarmed to look, craning over the shoulders of the pickmen.

The trench was close on a hundred and fifty feet wide, bounded on either side by towering walls of earth. That it revealed a section of the ancient palace was to be inferred from the fragments of brick pavement, the bases of a line of broken pillars deep bedded in the ground. In the side of the trench where the men were gathered, a fragment of wall, rising nearly ten feet in height, with a walled-up doorway, was visible. Merritt, arriving breathless, took command, restraining too ardent impatience on the part of the workmen. Carefully the earth was removed and the find laid bare.

"Looks like a tomb," said Holloway, leaving his camera and coming up. "Bricks, laid in bitumen, as usual. Hi! look out, you fellows! careful with your tools, there! There's an inscription over the door that you don't want to injure. Deane, bring your wisdom to bear on this."

"Scrape away the dirt, one of you," Merritt ordered; and a half-naked labourer sprang on the shoulders of a comrade and cleared away the clogging earth. Deane caught a sudden glimpse of Merritt's face and was reminded sharply of his outbreak of the night before. It was quite white with excitement, though his hands were steady, and his voice was cool. Then Deane, instantly alive with eagerness at sight of the carven words, took a careful copy of them in his notebook and hied himself away to decipher their meaning. Holloway placed his tripod in position, found the focus, and took an exposure of the wall and the low blocked-up doorway with its mysterious sign above. He was hot with excitement, as always upon such occasions, and begged strenuously that the door be instantly broken down.

"We have a couple of hours yet before it's too hot to work," Merritt observed. He pushed his helmet back and consulted his watch. "We'll make a beginning anyhow and keep it up as long as we can. From the appearance of the place, and the plan of what we've unearthed, I should say that this tomb, or whatever it was, must have been several feet below what was then the level of the ground. Got it already, Deane?"

Deane strolled up to the doorway, his pipe clenched between his teeth, his hat on the back of his head, and studied the inscription intently. Then he compared it with the copy he had made, and with various pages of his notebook. From time to time he mumbled unintelligibly. At last he turned upon them.

"I thought it was a tomb," he observed with satisfaction. "If I'm not mistaken, with this short time to go over it, the inscription says something like this: 'Whoso cometh, now or hereafter'—hereafter? —yes, that's right— 'wake not the soul that sleeps within.'"

"He must have wanted to sleep sound, whoever he was," Holloway observed with flippancy. "Can't we make a beginning? If the old man's still here, I'd like to collect him before it gets too dark."

Soon a force of men was at work, a swarm of ants prying around the edges of the walled-up door, where, above, the ancient message gave its warning. From this inscription Deane found himself unaccountably unable to keep his eyes. He and Holloway discussed it in low tones, to the accompaniment of the thud of falling pick and spade. Holloway wavered between the seductive idea of buried treasure, whose owner had perhaps sought to guard it with a theatrical warning, and the bejewelled mummy of the king he wished to collect. Deane hoped there would be tablets to decipher; Merritt said nothing. When Holloway questioned, wishing his theories on the subject, Merritt answered shortly:

"I'm not expecting anything in these countries any more. It's the unexpected that turns up and floors you, no matter what you think you'll get."

"You're right about these countries!" quoth Holloway with sudden enthusiasm. "They don't follow the rules and regulations of Home. After all, I suppose there's no reason why queer things shouldn't happen in queer lands. You don't understand 'em—you can't understand 'em—but, my aunt! don't they catch you right where you live sometimes! There's something about these Eastern lands that goes beyond the depth of a Westerner. It's in the very air of the place, and it's got into the people. I've knocked around some in India and Egypt and all that, but I know precious little more about them, except on the surface, than when I began. There's something that gets away from you; you can't get close enough to it to analyse it; you know it's there, but you can't give it a name. Even the little simple things seem somehow different. I've stood for hours outside a Buddhist temple, just listening to a woman praying that prayer of theirs— *'Om mani padme Hum!'* until I could almost fancy I was a Buddhist myself, praying with her. There's mystery all through it to me, and always will be. You see things and know them to exist, as well as you know anything, and can't account for them. And—well, once or twice I haven't seen things, but I knew they were there all the same. I think it must be what's behind all this—the past back of it, that makes it so deuced queer. Why, when I was in Darjeeling—"

But his audience melted away, and Holloway, his spirits nowise dampened by the curtailment of his reminiscences, went and helped the workmen dig, and sang their weird labour chants with them, with the harsh rattling chorus of pick and spade in them, and succeeded in infusing the men with his own overflowing enthusiasm, so that the work went on by strides.

The sun climbed higher, and the heat became great. Some of the men showed signs of exhaustion.

"We'll have to knock off for a while," Merritt said with reluctance. "It's ten o'clock already. Deane, better keep your hat on if you're going up. It's hot enough in the sun to give you a stroke in ten minutes."

Deane sat on the stump of a broken column and fanned his flushed face with his grey campaign hat.

"I've got a nasty headache on already," he admitted. "Hi! Ibraheem! Go to my tent, will you, and get the blue bottle out of my medicine chest. The blue bottle,

17

remember; it's the only blue bottle there. Put a spoonful in a cup of water and bring it here."

Ibraheem departed.

"Better try something a bit stronger," Merritt suggested.

Deane demurred.

"No; it's nothing but the beginning of a headache. Bromo will cure it quicker than anything."

Ibraheem returned shortly with the cup. Deane drank his dose, put on his hat, and went off among the workmen to watch the progress.

When a halt was called, the rubbish had been cleared away considerably, and some of the smaller bricks that blocked the entrance were out. Each man came up and peered solemnly through the gap, expressing disappointment when he saw nothing but blackness. Holloway created a mild sensation by declaring with his wonted vigour that he saw a pinpoint of light within. He was greatly chaffed, but stuck to his point manfully, even though he admitted that it "looked queer," and he could not at all account for it.

The men came filing up from the trenches to stretch themselves in the shade of the mounds. Holloway, being young and of indomitable enthusiasms, took himself off to develop his negatives, refusing to rest. Deane spread a mosquito net carefully over himself to keep off marauding flies, and went to sleep in the lee of the nearest mound. Merritt, pipe in mouth, sat where he and Deane had talked the night before, and stared out over the plain with sombre, thoughtful eyes.

As the burning day wore on, the ribald chatter of the natives ceased. They slept serenely while the shade lasted, making the most of their time of rest. When the sun, striding across the brazen sky, touched them where they lay, they woke, rose, moved in a body to fresh shelter, and slept again. Also the white men moved, in unison with them; Deane, half-awake, feverish with sleep, stumbling in his mosquito net. Where he fell he lay and slept again, breathing heavily, with restless turnings. In his dreams was a vast procession of brown-legged creatures who trailed endlessly up and down, coming from nowhere, going nowhere, who, each as it passed him, emptied a hod of dry brown earth upon him so that its weight pressed him down, and always down, into the earth, and shouted in his ears: "Whoso cometh, now or hereafter, let him not wake the soul that sleeps within!" Each voice grew louder and more menacing, though he could not understand why the brown creatures should threaten him; and as he tried to escape, they piled more earth upon him; so that, as he smothered to death, he woke with a gasp to find Holloway's hands heavy on his shoulders, and Holloway's voice crying:

"Get up, man! Oh, get up, I tell you! They've got the door down, and we're going in while the light lasts."

Deane jumped to his feet, his head still aswim, casting aside the mosquito net; and together they raced down the trench to where a crowd had gathered about a four-foot opening, yawning black. Nearest the entrance was Merritt, his face always pale with excitement, a shovel in his hands. He was as a detective who has found a clue to a tangled mystery—a miner who sees long-hoped-for signs of gold. Above his head the strange message blazoned forth its warning, the East guarding her secrets, even in death, from the eyes of the all-seeking West. To him it was never the routine of work, but the unfolding of a page whereon dead hands had traced the history of a vanished world. Over his shoulder he beckoned Deane and Holloway to him, stooping the while to peer into the low entrance. Before this was a mass of rubbish, with the bricks which had been removed

"Look in there!" he exclaimed. His words snapped like a whiplash. His eyes were keen and eager. "Does either of you see a—a light?"

Instantly they craned closer. Deane said:

"A what?"—and glanced at Merritt apprehensively; Holloway ejaculated:

"A—light!" in incredulous italics.

But then Holloway, gazing within, clutched Deane beside him, and said shrilly:

"It is! By George, it is! Didn't I say I saw a gleam when the first break was made, and didn't you rot me for it? But, oh, my Lord! how could a light get in there, fifty feet below the ground!"

"A reflection of outside light on something burnished within," Deane suggested at random.

Merritt lighted his lantern. "We'll have time to take a look," he said, quietly enough. "It's in a first-class state of preservation—the first chamber we've found not crushed in and filled with rubbish. Come along, you two, but bring your lamps."

He picked his way through the débris, and lifted one leg over the stone which formed the threshold, flinging the light of his lantern ahead. Deane and Holloway followed close upon his heels. The three stood within the tomb. Earth and stone had done what might be done to hold the secret given to their keeping, but man had conquered. The grave of the past was giving up its dead.

Before them was a short passage, not high enough for them to stand erect, slanting sharply downward, and turning to the right a rod ahead. The angle of the wall hid what lay beyond. By the light of the three lamps, which cast itself into the blackness, it could be seen that walls and roofs were of great blocks of stone, roughly hammer-dressed.

"I expected to find it caved in," came Holloway's voice from the background. "Think of the pressure on top."

"Yes; but this was deep underground in the beginning. The intermediate layer of earth must have helped support the mass which gradually formed above. Besides, it would take a——"

It was then that Deane, somewhat in the lead, turned the corner of the passage, and gave back upon them with a gasp and an oath, cutting Merritt's speech in two.

"There's something queer about this!" he muttered.

The turn of the passage led on a level a couple of yards farther. Here it was blocked by another entrance, likewise walled up. On a square stone beside this door stood a lamp of clay from which came, not a flame, but a pale radiance as from some material highly phosphorescent within, dim and feeble as though all but burned out. It was as though some living hand had placed it there but a little while before, behind those sealed-up walls, far down below the ground; a small atom of life, set in the midst of universal death, that smote them with an instant's shock as of something supernatural, not of earth.

Merritt said—"Good God! look at that!" below his breath, and halted, as one in presence of some power which had risen suddenly from the opened grave to mock at men. Confronting them thus, it was uncanny— a sentient thing with an individuality of its own. Deane, staring at it in fascination, said:

"It can't have been burning here these thousand years, ever since that outer door was bricked up—why, it's impossible. It's absurd. There must be some other way of entering. Someone must have been here before us."

They drew together, all three, and looked at it with wonder and with awe. The suggestion of it held them silent; the unexpectedness of it left them blank. Holloway, peering among the shadows, said abruptly:

"Turn your lanterns away a minute. Or shade them so the light won't fall ahead. So! Now!" His voice fairly shook with eagerness. "Look over the top of this door. There's an inscription—see? right over it—in big letters —and that lamp is placed precisely where it will throw light on it. That's why it is here—so that no one could possibly come to this door without seeing those letters. And when the light was brighter they must have been plain as print. Read 'em, Deane, quick."

Deane read, recognizing the word as one he had seen at times before. It was a single word:

"Forbidden."

But as they moved forward to look at it, the pale radiance, shining for untold years in that silent place, brightened in the wave of air they swept on with them, burned bravely an instant, and went quietly into nothingness. At once the clutch of death, held a thousand years at bay by its faint spark of life, settled heavily on the place. Merritt gave an exclamation of bitter disappointment.

"This must be where the old king lies," Holloway observed. "Shall we try it now? See here; these stones aren't one-fifth as heavy as those outside. I—by George! Here's one I can move. It might as well be dark as daylight, because we'll have to work with lanterns anyhow. I'll call up Ibraheem."

Ibraheem came, with two men and weapons of attack. The passage was too narrow to admit of more than two working at once; as it was, they were cramped for room and gasped for breath.

But by degrees, each man taking his turn, the door was broken out. Merritt, trimming his lamp afresh, stepped inside. Those waiting heard a stumble and a shout.

"Come in, you fellows! Bring lights. There's something here."

Promptly the two were after him. As they came, Merritt cried out sharply:

"Take care! You'll step on it! It's lying just inside the threshold."

Deane, entering first, threw his light ahead, and saw a thing huddled close to the door. Over it he stepped with care, and stooped beside Merritt to examine. Holloway, half in and half out of the low doorway, peered down at them; over his shoulder Ibraheem stretched his swarthy face.

"It's a mummy, sure enough," Holloway said, holding his light close. "But it's not wrapped in bandages, and it's not in any mummy-case. Just naturally dried up, I guess. Turn it over, Deane."

CHAPTER III

WITHIN THE TOMB

By now the lamps had steadied to brighter burning, so that the tomb was thrown into the light. It was low and square and very small; and around the walls were paintings, still more or less preserved, whose subjects they did not then stop to ascertain. Deane turned over the thing, shrivelled and brown and leathery, which once had lived and moved and breathed even as they themselves. Said Merritt:

"It's a woman. From the dress I should judge she was of high rank" —he whistled— "Look at the jewels!"

As the body was turned face upward, stiff as board, fixed to its crouching posture, the lamplight caught the flash of many jewels, the glint of gold, the dark fire of unknown gems. Around the shrunken neck was a chain of heavy links of gold; upon the shrivelled arms, long and bony, with claw-like hands, were broad, chased armlets, set with many jewels.

"It is in a remarkably fine state of preservation," Merritt said. He thumped hollowly with one finger on the sunken breast that had once been brown, smooth flesh, softly firm and dimpling to the touch; and held his light to the head. The hair was still attached to the skull, long, midnight black, straight and silky fine; but as he touched it, it came off in his hand. The eyes were gone, the sockets empty; the lips, dry and sunken, stretched grinning back from two rows of perfect teeth.

"What a mockery!" Merritt said suddenly. "I'd like to know what she was doing here. That door never got walled up in that style by any chance. Let's take a look around."

They looked; and on the walls they found their clue. The pictured story of a drama played out and ended direfully two thousand years before, with one of the actors, decked out as she had played her part, lying at their feet.

"I think it begins over here, where I am," Holloway remarked, from a corner near the door. "Where you are, they're walling up an entrance, and that must be pretty near the end. This first one here, where I'm standing."

They prowled around the walls, jostling one another in the smallness of the place, holding their lanterns close. Holloway, he of the ardent fancy, slapped his knee all at once with an exclamation.

"I've got it! At least it fits in with all the details we've found. She must have been of royal blood; for in that fourth picture she's with the man with the black beard, who has the symbol of royalty, and she's nearly as large as he. In this first scene she's making love to this duck in the white skirt, who is very much smaller, to show he's a mere man. He's coy, and has his hands before his face. I suppose that means he does not want to come into the game. Those three other fellows, who are lying on their backs over here, must have been three chaps who did not come to any good end by her. They all have their hands over their faces, you see; same position as the leading man. I guess she was a pretty strenuous lady, judging from these next two pictures. My word, they *are* frank, aren't they? In the fourth picture the king is reprimanding her for her ways, and she's got her back to him. On this wall, she's evidently being tried for her sins, and the king is pronouncing sentence. And here—hi! look at this—they're walling her up in this very tomb, alive. Here they're dragging her along that passage outside, with the tomb open and ready; and in this last one, the king is putting in a stone. There's the lamp standing on the stone block, with a slave doing something to it." He drew a long breath. "Well! by George! But why did they shut her up alive? Why didn't they poison her or cut her head off, or something that way?"

Here interruption came. Ibraheem, his keen-set curiosity overcoming even his superstitious awe of the place, came beside them to where the light fell full on the picture of the princess standing to receive sentence. Unexpectedly he yelled with surprise and alarm, and bolted for the door. Holloway caught him in midflight, demanding explanations.

"Saars, come away. Nis place so vurry wickit. Nat lady—what you call um Englis' devul soul. See—look."

He pointed to the painted figure. Merritt leaned forward to examine.

"This is quaint," he said. "See this thing that looks like a fancy ornament on her breast? It's no ornament; it's a little devil. And it's in every one of her pictures. You can see for yourselves."

"So it is," quoth Holloway, going around to investigate. "A little devil. Ain't it cute?"

But Ibraheem howled again.

"Nat um devul soul in she lookun out. Nat why she did got walled up. If she die so,"—he drew a hand across his neck,—"or get um killed, devul he get out of she and run away. Wall um up like nis so devul, when she die and he got out, mus' stay in here. Now you let devul soul out by opening wall. Come away queek."

Holloway laughed.

"Good eye, Ibraheem! We never thought we had such a glowing imagination in our midst. But I think myself we'd all better clear out. This air isn't any too sweet. And Deane's getting green around the gills some more."

From the workmen in the passage came a shout, and Ibraheem dived for the entrance.

"Say um roof come down!" he shouted as he fled. "Block up door. Come, saars!"

"Only some of the rubbish falling from above," Merritt said; but Holloway, already in retreat, called over his shoulder:

"You'd better hustle, you two! There's an avalanche coming down from somewhere."

He skipped over the threshold of the narrow door. Merritt, also bestirring himself, had got one leg over when there was a slide and a rattle; Holloway, Ibraheem, and the two workmen in the passage yelled in chorus, and Merritt jumped for safety. Then his place in the doorway was filled with a mass of loose earth and rough-hewn stones, entirely choking the entrance, and prisoning Deane on the wrong side.

They yelled again, encouragingly, to tell him that they would get right to work and dig him out; and their voices came to him indistinctly, as from a long distance. Holloway's lusty young shout, reaching him more clearly than the others', informed him that they would have him out in half an hour, and he might be philosophical and make love to the Princess to pass the time.

Deane smiled at his predicament, hearing the fall of pick and spade; a sound loud by comparison with the silence of the tomb. Then he became aware of how very silent it was. The stillness, which for unnumbered years had not been broken, seemed to grip the place again, overwhelming him, reclaiming its own. His one small lamp burned bravely, but the corners of the room were merged in shadow; the pictures on the walls loomed grotesque and indistinct. And then Deane's eyes fell upon the huddled mummy on the floor, and his imagination leaped back to what that last strange scene must have been. He thought of her, young perhaps, beautiful of course, thrust in there to perish by slow degrees, in the childish belief that the beautiful, evil soul of her, penned within the narrow walls, might never escape to wreak further havoc among the sons of men.

For some time he amused himself with such fancies, sitting on the floor, his hands clasped about his knees, his eyes on the jewelled mockery in the corner. Quite suddenly he became conscious of the heat and closeness of the place, and felt that a light sweat broke out on brow and hands; became conscious also of a certain mistiness in the tomb, in which the flame of his lamp glimmered wanly.

"I wish those fellows would hurry!" he muttered resentfully. He lifted his head abruptly, a new expression upon his face, his eyes agleam with an eager perplexity. "What in thunder is it? I thought I got a whiff of perfume—jasmine, by Jove!" Presently he shook his head. "Too elusive. Another freak of the sun; none of the fellows use scent and stuff—and as for the natives—" He broke off to chuckle. "Anyhow this place is getting confoundedly close." In the stifling atmosphere of the tomb he realised that his head was swimming curiously; his brain was dizzy, his hands grew cold. With a new inspiration, he said:

"Now, by Jove! I wonder if Ibraheem got hold of the right bottle?"

He became quite convinced that he had taken the wrong dose, and was filled with irritation against Ibraheem. He argued peevishly that it must have been the wrong dose, or he would not be feeling so uncommonly queer. Again his gaze fell on the mummy. This time he stared at it, his eyes fixed under frowning brows, his jaw dropping slightly. The light was dim, his head swimming. What he saw, watching in a fascination of interest, was a slow, indefinable change in the thing, which took place under his eyes, yet whose stages he could not follow. He saw the dead face turn slowly towards him—so slowly that, try as he might, he could not see it move—saw the sunken cheeks grow rounded, covered no longer with shrivelled parchment, but with velvety brown skin; saw full crimson lips which hid the twin rows of perfect teeth; saw the shrunken arms firm and gracious; the billowy curves and soft hollows of breast and throat, the sudden brilliancy of unknown jewels; and clutched his head in his hands.

"Gad! I'm getting light-headed!" he muttered. "It's the sun—of course it's the sun—it can't be anything but the sun!"

But he felt his flesh crawl to a sudden nameless horror which fastened upon him, like the horror of an evil dream which one knows to be a dream, but from which one cannot waken, when he knew that the vague sense of floating perfume was stronger, more clearly perceptible; the heavy, haunting scent of the jasmine flower, clinging and sensuous, and bringing with it a sudden ache of intolerable longing for the good life he had left behind.

"I don't understand!" he muttered. And then, aimlessly, and with a vague notion of having heard the words before, —"You see things, and know them to exist, and can't account for them."

Then he found himself all at once crawling on hands and knees towards the huddled figure that he knew watched him with living eyes, with the heavy fragrance of the jasmine luring him always on; and pulled himself up short with sudden terror in his face, believing quite seriously that he was mad, and shivering to think what might have occurred if he unwittingly had touched it. The light was dim and his eyes were full of mist, so that he could not see clearly; but he knew that it was lying very still, watching him with a sidelong under-glance, full of invitation and temptation, the jewels on rounded throat and curving breast winking in the light.

And then all power of will left him under the subtle, enervating fragrance that clutched at his brain and sent it reeling; and suddenly it became more than he could endure. He flung himself upon the earth and stones which filled the doorway, and tore at them, muttering rambling words beneath his breath, in a blind fear of something to which he could give no name.

Then a shout of men's voices struck his ears, close beside him; the air of the passage, pure and cool as heaven's own after the suffocation of the tomb, flooded him like a dash of cold water, infinitely grateful. He straightened himself, smiling vacantly, as Merritt and Holloway came towards him, and dropped in a heap just inside the threshold.

They carried him away with profane expressions of sympathy, and he raved half-consciously of dead things that watched him with living eyes; of flowers whose essence could drag a man's soul to the torments of the damned; and of the pain in his head, and of the sun, and blue bottles. And at the word, Ibraheem, quaking with fear, was fain to confess that in the medicine chest he could find no blue bottle and had brought instead a cup of plain water— "by Lord-God, saars, vurry plain!" —knowing the penalty of experimenting with drugs whose potency he did not understand.

And the tomb was left open to the clean night-winds, with Deane's forgotten lamp still burning on the floor, and casting its glimmer of light on the sunken face and the withered arms of the Princess with the mocking jewels who lay within.

CHAPTER IV

THE WOMAN TEMPTED ME

The camps settled down for the night, with occasional gusts of conversation from the men's quarters, —an altercation over a kettle of stew or a game of dice. Holloway strolled up to where Deane and Merritt sat smoking, after supper, his hands in his pockets, a cigarette between his teeth. Deane had a wet cloth bound around his head, and looked dissipated. Merritt was placid and thoughtful, resting contentedly in the memory of a good day's work behind him. This is greatly conducive to bodily and mental comfort at nightfall when the springs run down.

Holloway said casually:

"Which case have you packed the mummy in for shipment?"

"Haven't packed it at all yet," Merritt answered, tapping the bowl of his pipe against his boot. "There was no time to-day, between Deane's doings and the rest of it. It will be safe enough in the tomb until the morning. These Affejs would not touch it for unlimited backsheesh—and anyhow Ibraheem is on guard to see that they don't go monkeying around."

"Not packed it?" Holloway repeated. His voice held a faint inflection of surprise. "Well, it's not in the tomb. It's gone." Merritt straightened up and looked at him.

"How's that?" he demanded.

Said Holloway patiently:

"I thought you must have packed it, because it is not in the tomb. I was there not fifteen minutes ago. And Ibraheem was not there. He was eating his supper with—what's his name—Hafiz, the cooky. I'll bet those beggars have swiped it to loot the jewels."

Deane and Merritt answered nothing. Simultaneously they rose and made for the trenches. Holloway went after them leisurely, his hands in his pockets. Halfway down he met the two returning. Both were ejaculating profanely.

"Well?" said Holloway. "Was I right? Now there'll be the devil to pay."

"Right? Yes!" Merritt snorted. He gained the level, shouting for Ibraheem. The three seated themselves in solemn tribunal, out of earshot of the camp. Ibraheem came, serenely innocent. Merritt questioned, in the vernacular.

"You stood watch, Ibraheem, after we left the tomb?" His tones were honey-sweet.

"Ow yaas, saar." Ibraheem's voice was bland. Also he persisted in his English.

"For how long?"

"Ontil ne supper. My bellee he cry for goat-stew and cakes. Saars, he roar. So I went. Say I to me, eat a leetle bite and come back queek. Be not gone not long. I go; I am back queek. Not er minnut am I gone."

Merritt turned to Holloway.

"Was he there when you first went to the tomb?"

"No, sir!" Holloway answered promptly.

"How long were you there?"

"About an hour, as nearly as I can judge."

"Had he returned when you left? "

"No, sir."

Merritt's grey eyes transfixed Ibraheem, who quailed.

"While you were away from your post, in direct disobedience of orders, that mummy was stolen. Now it's up to you to find it. Do you understand, or shall I say it again in your lingo?" He repeated his words in the vernacular. "It shall be your business to find it. You shall question the men, examine the ground to see if it has been buried, look through all the camp. Until it is found, your wages are cut off. Also you get no backsheesh, and no gift when we return."

Ibraheem, prepared for anything save a loss of gold, became pitiable. His grief was childish; he wept, he implored forgiveness.

"I will find it, saar, mos' vurry damn queek. It is the men did got it, and from them I take it fierce. But give me gifts, or I die me dead of hongry. I am mos' poor men, vurry poor—I respectfully need gifts, saars!"

"Oh, stop your drooling and get to work!" Merritt growled, and turned his back on him. Ibraheem crept away, to fasten guilt, collectively and individually, upon every member of every gang. His progress through the camp was marked by a storm of wrathful protestations of innocence, of appeals to high Heaven for damaged reputations, of furious denials of complicity.

Merritt laughed shortly and lay down on his back.

"Don't you think all this rumpus might—er— frighten the thief into making off with the property?" Holloway wished to know.

"He couldn't make off very far," Merritt retorted grimly, and waved a hand at the surrounding desert. "If he tried it, we'd miss him from among the men, and be on him quicker than jumping. But it may scare him into quietly returning it, when he finds the secret is out."

But the next day the mummy of the Princess had not been returned, nor the next. Always the work went on, diligently, with varying success. More trenches were run deeper into the mound. Basketfuls of tablets were found, made of finest clay, many in a state of perfect preservation; also terra-cotta vases, instruments in copper, some corroded out of all shape; an altar to a god whose name had been erased, bearing marks of sacrifices. The courtyard of the palace was dug out, a wide and open space, with fragments of brick pavement and the remnants of its surrounding rooms. Of these architectural details Deane drew careful plans, noting their dimensions, the average height and thickness of their fragmentary walls, their drainage and ventilation. Squeezes were taken of inscriptions which could not be removed; the ground was carefully surveyed, the buildings photographed and described, preparatory to carrying the excavations to a lower level, where Merritt believed relics of a greater antiquity could be found. Again, other days were barren, and it was then that Merritt became sore over the loss of the Princess. When things went right he forgot her, in joy over some fresh acquisition; when things went wrong, he reverted to her, and mourned for her inconsolably.

"I was going to give the thing to the National Museum in Washington," he lamented bitterly. "And now, through the infernal greed of a fool of an Affej, it's lost. What's going without your dinner a time or two, when a thing like that is in the balance?"

But the fool of an Affej still held the centre of the stage, and was minded to make the most of it. Deane caught him one evening, purloining wax wherewith to plug up a gruesome gash, after the manner of desert surgery, and bound up the wound himself in proper style. So that Ibraheem, feeling himself sadly ill-used and outcast since the day of his disgrace, became grateful, and—always in his painful English—informed him that the night before a workman had disappeared, not returning with his gang at sunset, and that the man who had seen him last was in the camp, very sick.

All this Deane dutifully reported to Merritt, and Merritt grunted sleepily and said:

"The fellow's gone to sleep behind one of the mounds. He'll turn up in time for breakfast, never fear."

But he did not turn up in time for breakfast, and the sick man was sicker, and wished to die. Asked by curious comrades as to the cause of his distress, he replied that he would not tell, and did not wish to talk; so that he received scant sympathy, and his attendants dwindled. It was upon this night that Deane dreamed of being again a prisoner in the tomb, with the living eyes in the dead face watching him as he fought his way to air and life. Only this time the face seemed not all dead; the skin was brown and drawn tight across the bones, but in the face there was expression; lust and cruelty, and a triumph which was of evil. He woke bathed in sweat, with a feeling of suffocation such as had choked him on that unforgotten day in the airless tomb. For the first time he was struck with a sense of impending evil; though, when he woke again, this had vanished wholly in the brave morning light.

It was within a day of this that a certain uneasiness made itself manifest among the men. In the evening a deputation visited Merritt, and set forth their troubles at great length. They made Ibraheem their spokesman; he revelled in the chance of exploiting his English, and made the most of it.

"Saar Merritt will not forget nat it is accursed citee, accursed by Lord-God in vurry long time ago. Nere may be bad affairs, vurry bad, which we shall see. It is not good to unbury what is bad. Nare is a altar of so most wickit Lord-God which men says shine all night. Spucks are here—all, all around. We did got vurry great lot spucks in nis land. The mens don't not like him. Hafiz, he cook, see a ting, las' night. Make um vurry seek."

He pulled forth Hafiz by the tail of his short and dirty cotton garment. Hafiz was unwilling, but seeing himself surrounded, hearing himself bidden to speak, spread out his hands and said rapidly:

"It is a thing, oh, my masters, which comes from the mounds at night-time, swaying as the corn sways in summer, very light, beckoning men to follow. Tarfa, he who went and came not back, saw and said it is the god of that altar we have profaned. The desert has swallowed him; for it is three days since he hath gone." Then he called Allah to witness—for he was a good Mohammedan—that he intended no meddling with unseen things, that he was forced to obey orders, and that he was a flower in Allah's hands.

"I don't understand what's got into the brutes," Holloway said fretfully.

"They're just a bit nervous," Merritt assured him. "It seems as though this place always had a bad name, from the earliest times. The men are superstitious, and they don't know exactly what they're up against. _I_ think Tarfa is responsible for the mummy, and invented the tale of the shining altar before he left, to throw us off the track. Yes, he's undoubtedly the thief. But he wouldn't be such a fool as to cross northward without water or provisions—and cooky says he took nothing from the stores and the only other practicable route would be southward. So when we go back that way, we'll find him—or what's left of him—and it."

"But the Rocks? Suppose he makes for them?" Deane suggested.

At this idea, however, Merritt scoffed.

"Why should he go there? His main wish, I take it, would be to get into the track of caravans, where he might find help. He'd throw the mummy away in the desert, and hide the jewels in his shirt. Among the Rocks, he might as well go north and be done with it.

No caravans pass within fifty miles of the place, and then rarely; and fifty miles is no joke to an exhausted man without food or water. Oh, we'll get the Princess back yet!"

The next day came a flurry of disturbance. A digger came to Merritt and told him, quite hysterically, that he, Moussa, had seen a man slipping away among the mounds, following a thing which went always on ahead; and the man was Hafiz, the cook, who had been with Tarfa and had later wished to die. And Moussa, shuddering, told what the thing was, as he had seen it.

"Master, it was near to dark, and I and Hafiz took food and went to the shade of that mound and ate." He waved his hand at a hill of upturned earth and rubbish at a distance upon the left. "And just as the sun sank, in that moment before night fell, there came a breath of air from the gardens of the blessed souls in Paradise, slow and soft as the whisper of women's voices, and It came, slowly, around the mound, and looked upon Hafiz, and beckoned. And the desert was no longer a desert, but as a garden filled with the scent of roses and the song of bulbuls. And it was a woman, master, as Allah lives, a woman, here in this place, where a woman had not been before, and her eyes were dark and her mouth red. She stood swaying just in the shadow of the earth, and beckoned; and I cried out in fear, but Hafiz would follow. And when I would have held him back, he cursed me, and went, following that woman who laughed and beckoned, for the sweetness of her was in his nostrils, and her will was to be obeyed. And when I, fearing greatly, went around also, I could not see them, for the darkness of night had come. Eh, masters, but she was beautiful, and very evil, and her jewels were such as none had ever seen before upon the earth."

Merritt turned sharply upon Ibraheem, who stood behind him.

"Did I not tell you that liquor was *not* to be brought along for the men? By Jove! we'll have them seeing sacred pythons and jumping lizards next!"

"Not got um liquor, saar," Ibraheem interrupted. "Not um drop er whiskey in er camp. Sun touch um here."He tapped his forehead significantly. Merritt grunted in unbelieving disgust.

That night the three sat late, unwontedly silent, watching the desert night and the pulsing stars. Holloway was the first to break a pause of many minutes.

"These men aren't children, to be scared of shadows. I think this thing ought to be sifted. And when you come to think of their point of view, this is a pretty weird sort of a place. There's a-plenty to cook up a rattling good ghost story out of; this old cursed city, the altars to unknown gods where human sacrifices were offered; that mummy Princess, with her 'devil-soul' and her jewels and her story painted on the walls of her own tomb; and now the disappearance of our men, one by one. Well, I'm glad you two fellows are here, anyhow. If I were alone, by George, I shouldn't wonder if I'd get to believing in Ibraheem's spucks myself. I'd end by cutting loose and running away."

Deane smiled at the boy through a cloud of tobacco smoke; and Merritt said, with a dry affection which only Holloway, with his spirits, his light-heartedness, and the unexpected contradiction of an imagination more torrid even than Merritt's own, could wring from him:

"Oh, yes! I have seen you run like that before, you young dare-devil. They'll forget about all this in a couple of days. They merely think it's their duty not to let one trip go by without stirring up something sensational."

Holloway sighed portentously.

"Well, you can search me!" he said with frankness. "I give it up. This country gets beyond the depth of my philosophy. Upon my soul, if I stay here much longer, I'll be ready to believe anything you tell me of it."

CHAPTER V

A TOUCH OF THE SUN

A day later Ibraheem reported that Moussa had taken himself off. Ibraheem was nervous, and showed it. The men were getting restless, he averred; he himself would be glad when the work in that place was finished. It was an unholy spot. Furthermore, he declared that he had seen Moussa the night before, and Moussa had behaved peculiarly, had talked of rose gardens and strange perfumes to which no man could give a name, and had said that if he saw the Woman again he was determined to follow her. Wherefore Moussa was undoubtedly mad, Ibraheem said with great solemnity, for Lord-God knew there were no women around that camp, neither was there any perfume save the reek of the cattle-pen. Oh, yes—Moussa was mad, most mad, there was no doubt whatever about that. In consequence of this, Merritt ordered a search made for concealed liquor, and found none. The men watched the proceedings in silence. That night there was no singing; men gathered close and slept in bunches of three and four.

Some hours later, Deane, on his way to his tent, stumbled over Holloway, who sprawled upon the ground, chin on hands.

"Look out!" Holloway said mildly, not offering to move. "I say, look at that moonrise."

His voice had lost some of its enthusiasm, and sounded tired. Deane, considering that the boy was homesick and perhaps needed bracing up, accepted the implied invitation, and sat down. The moon, climbing over the great Mound of the City, was turning the sky to intense blue-black; the earth to a slumbering sea of hoary light, wrapped in infinite loneliness and peace.

"It's bully," Deane assented unheedingly. Quickly it became plain to him that moonrises, usually conducive to poetic enthusiasms on Holloway's part, to-night held no attraction for him. He, generally brimming over with life and spirits, was suddenly distrait and listless. Deane was wondering if by any chance the boy had exposed himself to the sun, when Holloway spoke, with a certain hesitancy and constraint which had the effect of making him appear all at once more than ever boyish.

"Deane, do you know I've been wondering if there could be anything in those fellows' stories, after all? I don't mean any of that rot about a woman, but ...I saw something myself to-night."

"Where?" Deane asked with equal seriousness. The darkness hid a smile of amused tolerance on his face.

"Down among the tombs." Holloway's voice was solemn.

"Perhaps a goat got loose," Deane suggested hopefully.

"Oh, you can laugh if you like!" Holloway said with unexpected emphasis. "Of course, you'll say next it was one of the men. It might have been, but I'll take my oath it wasn't. Why should they be sneaking 'round there at that hour, when they wouldn't go near the place after dark to save their immortal souls?"

"Why were you there?" Deane queried.

At Holloway's reply, low, and with an odd note of breathlessness in it, he straightened up in the darkness, trying to see the other's face.

"I don't know. I'm—I'm all sorts of a fool, but—I can't keep away from the place somehow. I tell you, Deane, I've been there every night for the last four nights, and I'm afraid as death of it."

"Then, in Heaven's name, why do you go?" Deane asked amazedly.

"I tell you I can't help it!" Holloway answered with quick impatience. "Before I know it, I'm there. I say, Deane, when people have a touch of the sun, does it make 'em see things that—well, that aren't there, you know?"

"I don't know," Deane said slowly, and stopped, remembering a picture, always with him, of a dim-lit tomb, of a jewelled thing with flaming eyes that crouched upon the floor, of himself, half senseless, dizzy with the dreaded sunsickness, digging with naked hands at the fallen earth in an agony of idiotic fear.

"Yes, it does," he said decidedly.

Holloway drew a long breath of relief. "Thank Heaven for that! If I hadn't that excuse I'd think I'd got 'em, sure enough.... What a jolly night this is! like some of the nights we have at Home, in late spring." He stretched his muscular length comfortably, in relaxed content, staring upward at the poising moon. Deane, seeing that he was talking off, in his own way, the vague unrest which had held him, gave him his head, paying not much attention to his idle words. "There's a hill behind the old house," the boyish voice went on. "The moon comes up behind it just as it comes up behind the Mound of the City every night. And there's a big old apple-tree there, and right below is the garden where the violets grow. I've been smelling those violets all day—seems as though I could look down any minute and expect to see them growing in the warmth and dampness. Funny thing how a fellow can almost make himself believe he's smelling flowers when there aren't any flowers in a thousand miles, and how the mere remembrance of the perfume will bring things back to him that he'd forgotten long ago. I don't know how I got to imagining all that, but it had quite a curious effect on me; made me want that little old bull-pup of mine as I never thought I'd want anything again in this weary world. I'd give half I've got to have him here now, with his head on my knee; and I don't quite know why, because violets haven't much to do with bull-terriers."

Deane came out of his reverie, conscious only of the fact that Holloway was still speaking.

"What's that?" he demanded.

"I was just talking about Keno, my dog," said Holloway plaintively. "This moon made me think of the old garden back home, and the violets growing there—I swear I can almost smell 'em now—and one thing and another made me think of that pup of mine. He's about the only one I've got to think of now. Go to sleep again—don't mind me. I wonder if it's one of the phases of this beastly sunsickness. If it is, I've got a touch, sure."

"Is what one of the phases?" Deane queried sleepily, as Holloway paused, expectant of an answer.

"The—er—smelling perfumes that aren't there and that sort of thing—why, what's the matter?"

Deane sat up and laid a hand on Holloway's arm and shook him gently.

"Have you been doing that, too?" he demanded. "See here, Bob, have you been doing that, too?"

"Yes, I have, in a sort of a way," Holloway admitted. "I didn't know there was anything to jar you in that. It's part of the regular programme, isn't it? —headache, pain in the back of the neck, red-hot iron band across the eyes, smelling things and seeing things of various sorts. Is it a—a symptom? It must be—what else in thunder could it be? I don't know that I mind it so much; it isn't unpleasant, in a way, but—oh, I don't know! It made me so damnably homesick—"

He stopped on the word and moved uneasily in the darkness.

"I'm talking rot," he said firmly. "Guess that's a symptom, too. Well, I believe I'll turn in."

He eyed his own tent, standing farthest off, white in the moonlight.

"Better take yourself in hand and get rid of these attacks," Deane advised him kindly. "The sun is not a thing to be treated lightly in these parts, you know."

As Holloway moved away, slowly, he watched him with narrowed eyes. Then he went into his own tent and lighted his lamp. With his leather trunk for desk, he wrote up his notes, and arranged his journal and books of entry; while outside the night deepened and all the camp slumbered.

Later he put away his papers, and prepared for bed. As he stretched out a hand to extinguish the lamp, he stopped suddenly, head bent, listening intently. On the other side of the wall, close against the canvas, was a small sound as of a heavy body which had brushed against it in rolling over. Deane removed his boots, and went noiselessly to the door. He peered through the flap into the moonlight; abruptly drew back with a quick intake of breath.

"Good Lord!" he muttered. "That boy!... Camping down here in one

blanket instead of sleeping decently in his tent.... Is the youngster crazy?"

An instant he thought rapidly. He drew on his boots, bestirred himself briskly a moment, making much noise; and listened again then called out in natural tones:

"Hello, Holloway! Not turned in yet? Come in."

And grinned as he heard a confused movement of surprise on the other side of the tent-wall, then a step.

"Come on in," he invited heartily. "Flap's loose"; and bent over his journal assiduously.

Holloway entered, and Deane faced around, levelling a keen glance at him.

"Sure I won't disturb you?" Holloway asked; and at the tone of his voice Deane's glance became keener.

"Not at all," he answered. "Fact is, I'm glad you came. I heard—er—your step passing, and thought I'd get you to come in. Do you happen to remember which case the squeeze of the Library inscription was packed in?"

"I—don't believe I do," said Holloway. He dropped down on a camp-stool. "Deane, can't you give me something to make me sleep? I'm—I'm no good at all to-night. It's the sun—of course it's the sun."

Deane looked at him, frowning a little with perplexity. He sat tensely, gripping the edge of the camp-stool with both hands. His face was pale, his fair hair wildly rumpled. His jaws were set, but from time to time the corners of his mouth twitched. On one shoulder was a long smear of earth. All at once he turned restive under Deane's eyes.

"Oh, cut it off!" he cried querulously. "It's nothing but the sun, I tell you. If I could get one night's sleep I'd be all right."

"I'll give you a dose," Deane said, and went to the medicine chest by the head of his bed. Over his shoulder he added, watching keenly the effect of his words—"Only you'll have to camp down here with me till morning. So that I can watch its effect, you understand."

The change in the boy's face was swift and sharp, but Deane caught it; a look of utter relief, a certain quick relaxing of the tension. Holloway said with eagerness:

"Can I?" and caught himself up to add: "Oh, but I'm afraid it'll be beastly inconvenient for you."

"Don't let that worry you," Deane returned, and went on with his preparations. From their net he took half a dozen limes, and into a tin cup poured cool water from the porous water-jar which hung at the tent door. He squeezed the lime-juice into this, added a scant allowance of sugar and a dash from a blue bottle, and shook the whole up in a mixing-glass.

"That wouldn't hurt an infant," he said with satisfaction. "Human companionship is all the medicine the poor devil wants this night." He turned to Holloway suddenly. "Here, old man," he said—and saw that Holloway jumped at his voice as though he had been shot—"drink it slowly. It will help things along some, I think."

Holloway took the cup, with thanks and high faith in its sleep-inducing properties, and sipped docilely. Deane made sundry preparations, whistling softly through his teeth. The lamplight cast grotesque shadows behind him as he moved.

"Now, get yourself to bed as quick as you know how," he ordered. "In ten minutes you'll be asleep and warranted not to dream."

"But where are you going to sleep?" his patient asked, rising.

"Never mind about me," Deane said with decision.

Still docile, Holloway got himself to bed, drawing the blanket to his chin. He gave a long sigh of comfort, as he watched Deane moving to and fro, like a child that feels itself secure against unknown terrors of the dark in the company of its elders. Deane rolled himself in his blanket on the floor in a position so that he could keep Holloway in view, tucked his coat under his head as pillow, and started to turn out the lamp. But Holloway sat suddenly bolt upright in the bed, and began to speak rapidly, in a high voice:

"Deane, hold on a minute! I might as well make a clean breast of it. I'll be damned if I impose on you like this. I'm not sick; there's nothing the matter with me except sheer beastly funk. I don't know how you thought you heard me passing outside. The truth of it is, I was curled up in a blanket on the other side of this wall, where I could hear you moving in here and the scratch of your pen. All I wanted was to be within range of somebody, where I could hear somebody moving, and know I wasn't alone with It. I knew if I stayed in my tent an hour longer I'd be off down among those tombs again. I was afraid, utterly afraid and you can guess if it's a pleasant thing to own up to but 'fore God I don't know what I was afraid of. I didn't intend to come in here and rout you out like this. Just let me have a blanket and a place on the floor—I don't want your bed."

He flung off the blankets and put a foot on the floor. Deane rolled out of his own blanket, sprang to his feet, and forced him back again.

"You stay right where you are, Bob. This business has got on your nerves a bit, that's all. Man alive! don't worry about the bed. Hope you don't think it's the first time I've slept out of one! And I'm jolly glad you came to me if you felt like that about it. It's not a good thing for a fellow to be alone when he begins to get floored this way. Now go to sleep, will you?"

Holloway subsided. Deane went back to his corner and lay down. There was a long silence. Unexpectedly Holloway said in matter-of-fact tones from the depths of his blankets:

"I say, this is a hell of a place, isn't it?"

CHAPTER VI
THE ONE WHO WENT AWAY

In the morning, when Deane awoke, he found his patient departed. At breakfast, in the grey dawn before sunrise, Holloway appeared, exceedingly dignified, carefully unconcerned. Deane showed wisdom by making no allusion to what had gone before; so that, by degrees, Holloway's dignity relaxed.

During the morning, Deane spent most of his time in carefully packing cases of antiquities for safe transportation. Merritt, as usual, was in the trenches with his men; Holloway took photographs indefatigably. He swore quite savagely at his boy when the latter spilled a pan of fixative; and this was a thing unusual to Holloway's blithe good temper. Later, he and Deane fell out, over a question whose seriousness at one time threatened to plunge all three into civil war. Deane opened the fray by declaring, *à propos* of dinners, that the only proper way to create a cocktail of the genus Martini was to add a half-spoonful of sherry after the other ingredients had been satisfactorily mixed, if at all. Holloway declared with vigour that the sherry should go in before the vermouth, in order to blend properly; and announced that he would concoct a specimen on this plan for Deane at the Waldorf the night they reached New York, and stand him a champagne supper if his theory failed. They argued warmly; Merritt, rashly undertaking to mediate, was speedily placed *hors de combat* and forced to retire ignominiously. The contestants waxed eloquent in invective, losing sight completely of the *casus belli*; in the end they parted, sulky as two angry children; thereafter ignored each other in high disdain. Merritt, sorely perplexed, strove to pour balm into their wounds, with assurances that both were right—that either way was equally good, and that the sun was responsible for their—er, irritation. Whereat Holloway retorted that the sun had nothing whatever to do with it—that it was merely the obstinate pigheadedness of some people who could see no other point of view than their own. To this Deane replied that it was not even this, but—and stopped short. So that Holloway, imagining a taunt where none was meant, glared at him in fury and strode away.

"Now, what's got into him?" Merritt exclaimed, half-irritated, half-amused.

"I guess he imagines I was going to twit him with something that happened—er, once," Deane answered lucidly. "He ought to be taught not to go around with a chip on his shoulder. It's disgusting bad form. I never would have thought of arguing with him if he had not taken the words out of my mouth."

He was very busy all that afternoon. Occasionally, over his lists and identification-slips, he found time to grin somewhat sheepishly at the futile squabble; also for a faint patronising resentment at what he was pleased to term Holloway's crudeness.

At supper Merritt glanced around as though all at once missing something, and said:

"Where's Holloway?"

Deane helped himself to canned apricots, and answered tolerantly:

"Still sulking, I suppose. He doesn't usually go off the tether like this. I always thought him a pretty good-natured sort of cub."

"So he is!" Merritt answered. "Seems to me you were a bit rough on him, Deane. The sun in these parts has a trick of upsetting a fellow once in a while, and the boy isn't seasoned timber yet.—Now about that 'perpetual lamp.' I shall give it to Dr. Peabody, at the Museum in Washington, with a written description of the circumstances under which it was found. I haven't touched it, beyond packing it away in the D case. He can extract whatever is inside. It may solve, or help to solve, the problem which men have been working over a good many years—the secret of perpetual light. I wish it to go on exhibition, with some of the tablets and vases, when our men are through with them. How are the squeezes coming on?"

They smoked peaceful after-dinner pipes, and talked over their plans and projects. At times Deane caught himself listening for a quick, boyish step and an outbreak of cheerful slang.

When the next morning's work was under way, Deane, wishing an exposure made of a certain patterned pavement, that the photograph might aid in replacing the numbered pieces when the bit was reconstructed, went for Holloway and his camera. Merritt had got to work earlier than usual that morning; he could hear him shouting from one trench to Ibraheem in another. Abruptly he came upon him, and full of the business in hand, demanded:

"Where's Holloway? I want him to get a shot at the pavement in Square 14."

Merritt glanced at him with a sudden gravity.

"Didn't you know? Holloway did not come back to camp last night. I've got a couple of men out now hunting him among the tombs. He must have fallen down and injured himself. Perhaps a tunnel caved in on him somewhere."

The shock of this announcement turned Deane cold. Uppermost in his mind was the thought—"Two gone! What if the boy should be the third?"

"Oh, he—he's around here somewhere," he said, and strove to speak lightly. Merritt pushed his hat on the back of his head with a gesture full of worry and bewilderment.

"I hope so!" he said slowly. "Of course, it must be so. But...there are Tarfa and Hafiz, you know!"

"Perhaps he came back, and went away so early that we did not see him," Deane suggested. At heart he knew this to be futile. Merritt shook his head.

"No, I asked Hamd, his boy." He braced himself visibly against a certain depression, a premonition of hopelessness. "They may bring him in at noon," he said, with an obvious effort at cheerfulness. "If not—well, we'll send out more men. I'm afraid he's had a touch of the sun lately, to tell the truth. He's such a worker, and so willing to take any job that comes his way, that I— half the time I forget he's green, and ought to have an eye kept on him, and take it out of him more than he can stand, I'm afraid. And he'd go till he dropped, the beggar, and never open his mouth. That's the worst of him; I can't tell when he's done up. Oh, yes; he'll come in with the men at noon, sure."

They cheered themselves with this refrain throughout the afternoon. But towards evening Merritt's grey face was greyer and greatly worn, and Deane was silent and very thoughtful. Candidly he confessed that he had been a brute; had he also got a touch of the sun? His mind went back to the scene in his tent the night before; he heard the high, boyish voice, keyed to nervous confession, saying: "All I wanted was to be within range of somebody, where I could hear somebody moving.... I knew if I stayed in that tent alone an hour longer, I'd be off among those tombs again.... I cannot keep away from the place.... I've been there for the last four nights, and I'm afraid as death of it." He lost himself in a maze of vain imaginings. Had the boy wanted him last night—needed the support of human companionship, and not come to him because of their foolish squabble, fearing scorn and ridicule? Had he fought off his madness by himself, hour after hour in the darkness, and at last given way and wandered into the place he dreaded—and what had happened then? Deane knew that imagination is a terribly real factor in certain crises of life, let it but get its grip upon its victim. And Holloway...at the thought that he might be following in the footsteps of those other two, vanished utterly from the face of the earth, Deane started up to pace the camp in an agony of restlessness.

Ibraheem, scorching himself before the fire in devoted tendance of a covered dish containing dainties saved from supper for the return of Holloway, whom he loved, looked up at Deane's sudden motion.

"Ne master have send out more man," he said mournfully.

Deane nodded. Ibraheem nursed his dish.

"Saar, I ask a word, mos' respectful. What nis go to mean. What is eraisho-uf-perluserpy?"

Deane pondered.

"Give it up! Where did you hear that?"

"Mister Holloway said um. To me. Las' night. I am sit by fire. He come walkun queek; see me and stop. He say, 'Ibraheem, it is late, eh?' I say vurry late. He say, 'Ibraheem, I have saw her, ne woman what is a what you call *jinn*.' Jus' lak nat."

"The woman! That empty superstition again!" Deane groaned.

"I say, 'Saar, for Lord-God sake don't not go. Come queek and lie in bed.' And he say, 'Oh, I'm not goin' after her, you old fool. Jus' goin' down in tombs a leetle.' Nen he laugh and say, 'Nere is more affair in Heaven-Earth eraisho nan in er perluserpy'—I don't know what else. Some kind dam' bad Englis' nat, eh? So he go, and byumby I go to hole and look down for to see um. But I see um comin' to me, on ne ground, saar, all white in she face, wiv um eyes green lak fire, sleepin' round mound-earths lak um cat at night, sayin' so sof': 'I won't not go—I won't not go.' Nen he go, and I run queek to ne mens and fall down, and go to slip to keep um spucks away."

Deane went off to Merritt.

"I'm going to look for the boy myself. If what Ibraheem says is straight, I'm afraid he's gone as Tarfa and Hafiz went."

Merritt looked at him.

"You mean——"

Deane nodded miserably.

"Yes. It seems he saw the same thing. Ibraheem heard him talking."

"Why didn't Ibraheem stop him?" Merritt cried with a flash of anger.

"Oh, because he's a fool," Deane retorted. "I shall take half a dozen men, with food and all the water you can spare. Somehow—" he drew a long breath, setting his teeth— "I feel as though it had been partly my fault. You see—a couple of nights ago he came and told me a thing or two. And I shouldn't have spoken as I did yesterday. I ought to have remembered." Suddenly he struck one fist into the palm of his open hand. "Oh, it's impossible!" he cried harshly. "Nothing so hellish could happen! He must be around somewhere; surely we'll overtake him in a couple of miles! I wish to Heaven we'd never set eyes on this cursed place!"

Two hours later Deane and his party started. Deane, the last to leave, came to Merritt and held out his hand.

"Good-bye," he said. "Will you run up a flag on the tallest pole on the highest mound, and leave it there until we get back?"

Merritt's hand gripped his—hard.

"Aye," he said. "I'll do it. God grant you bring the poor lad back safe with you. But...take care of yourself, Deane. Remember that if you don't find him within the week, it...will be no use to look further."

They rode away towards the darkening east, away from the sunset; and he watched, without speech or motion, until they were mere black dots crawling upon the desert floor.

Thereafter, Merritt discovered that he had fresh troubles on his hands. The fourth day after Deane's departure a man raced into the camp at supper-time, crying shrilly. His words brought the camp about him, nervous, ready for any new alarm. Ibraheem dragged him to Merritt, leaving a tumult of excited voices in his wake; and reported that the man, returning to the farthest trench after the workmen were gone, to look for a lost pick-head, had found the mummy of the Princess in a shallow cave in a heap of rubbish. Ibraheem further stated that the men demanded instant permission to wall it up in its tomb again, that the evil spell of the place might thus be broken.

Merritt was surprised and amused and indignant. The finding of the mummy was a big piece of luck; the man should be rewarded. But as for burying it again, that was not to be thought of. It was entirely senseless for the men to connect that bit of harmless dried skin and bones with all their troubles; such a theory was not worth serious consideration. The mummy should be recovered and packed securely that same night. Also the finder was to go with Merritt at once to point out its whereabouts. In vain the man protested. Merritt's grey eye overawed him; he yielded and went, first borrowing all the amulets he could find from any who would lend. Thus equipped and fortified against the Devil, he led the way, shivering and whining, past the trenches nearest the camp to one of the old diggings. Here he searched until he came to a shallow cave in the further side of the rubbish-heap.

"This is the place, my master," he said, and crept forward to look. Then he dropped upon his knees and felt for all his amulets and prayed crazily, even as Merritt said with sternness:

"You've forgotten the place. There's no mummy here."

"But it is the place, my master, where one hour ago my eyes did see it. By Allah, it is the place! It has gone, and because I tracked it, its wrath shall come upon me, and I shall perish as did my master and my friends. Oh, master, come away! The place is cursed. It is the lair of the evil soul, which we have freed from death to lure us into death. Ai, master, come!"

"Get along with you, you chicken-heart!" Merritt muttered in wrathful Anglo-Saxon, and waved him off. The man knew not the words, but took the hint and fled. For an hour Merritt patiently searched the mounds, the abandoned trenches, the deserted tombs. Once he looked up, feeling eyes upon him, and said with annoyance:

"Get back to camp, I tell you! If you won't work, I won't have you peering around here." Again, later, he repeated his command, with growing anger. In the end he found nothing, and became convinced that the man had lied. He marched back to camp, hot and much disgusted, and sent for the culprit, who came in serene innocence.

"Why did you lie to me?" Merritt asked. "When I sent you from the place, why did you return? So that you might laugh when you saw that I followed your worthless directions?"

"I was not from the camp, my master!" the man declared. "And where I said I saw the mummy, there I saw it. When it went I do not know; where it went I do not know either."

"That'll do. Perhaps you don't. Only bring no more fairy tales here. I won't have 'em. Understand?"

But in the morning a new complication rose. Ibraheem hunted up Merritt, an uneasy scowl on his dark face, and told him that the men absolutely refused to enter the trenches. The workman's tale had done its business. They were afraid, they acknowledged frankly; they would do anything under heaven to please their master, whom they loved as they loved their fathers and their mothers, but enter the accursed city and its devil-haunted tombs, they would not. Merritt saw that unless he played his cards with care, he would have a mutiny upon his hands. Superstition was rampant; they were an hundred, he was one. Only the workman who had given the false alarm stuck to Merritt. For three days the two laboured, doing what two pair of willing arms might do; for three days the army of shirkers ate and loafed and smoked and slept in the shade, embarrassingly respectful to Merritt, stubborn as polite mules when it came to the test.

Then the devoted one disappeared, even as three before him had done, in the night, in silence and mystery. This raised an open panic. The men became utterly convinced of an influence for evil working actively in their midst; each man looked upon himself as the next possible victim. Ibraheem hinted to Merritt that they might, in an excess of terror, capture the animals and provisions and desert in a body, taking the law into their own hands; and Merritt leaped from his camp-chair and strode out into the sunlight, his jaw set, his eyes ablaze with the light of coming battle. The men, gathered into muttering groups, drew apart as he appeared among them. He seized the instant's advantage their pause gave him and spoke, not loudly, not angrily, but so that every man heard his voice, and felt his courage oozing from him under the fire of the grey Saxon eyes. His words were Arabic, and understood by all; he stood upon a hillock of rubbish, bareheaded, his shirt blowing free from his tanned neck, head thrown back, unarmed, dominating them by sheer force of will and the heritage of the blood that was in him.

"See here, men, you're not children to be frightened at the dark like this. Queer things have happened lately, I'm not denying, but they're queer only because we have not happened to hit on the right explanation of them. Don't you know that yourselves?" One or two heads nodded doubtfully. "I'm not going to argue with you; I'm not even going to tell you that you're fools. In regard to Daheer, who went away last night—how do you know but that one of your own number, in revenge for his faithfulness to me, frightened him in the night-time, so that he, thinking the hand of evil was upon him, fled into the desert to escape?"

They did not know. Quickly they saw his point—an Arab is not slow-witted—and discussed it among themselves. Each knew that himself had not done it— that went without saying—but whether another was guilty they could not tell.

"Whoever will may leave this place," Merritt said; and at once there was a turning of heads towards him. "But he must go without food and without water, since I do not intend to equip any personally-conducted expeditions. If he will, let him go from here westward, where in four days, or five, at most, he shall come into the track of caravans. If he is lucky he may find a caravan passing, and receive food and drink. If he finds no caravan, then...it may be that he will wish that he had stayed with me." He paused, to let this idea sink home.

"But whoever stays with me" —his voice deepened —"shall work in the trenches or out of the trenches, as I command. I will have no shirking, no complaints. For two days I have waited to see if wisdom would enter you; now I wait no longer. Choose now; will you go or stay?"

A gasp of astonishment followed his words. They had expected time to make up their minds, and in the East time means eternity. To be put to the question thus, brutally, at once, was unexpected. They wavered, chattered, became all at once helpless and vacillating. Merritt spoke once more.

"If you go, you are free to wander as you like, and to perish as you like. But if you stay you will obey my orders without question, will answer fully and completely to my commands; for I am the master here!"

His voice held menace and power and warning. They murmured. Merritt's eyes flashed; he sprang from the low hillock of earth. He was unarmed, but they shrank back. And it was then that a sound broke in upon them; and Ibraheem, wheeling to look, cried aloud, and ran to Merritt and shook his arm, shouting:

"Look—see, saar! Oh, Lord-God, look see!"

Behind them, so that they turned to see it, a figure was racing over the sands rapidly, stumbling with staggering steps, a gaunt skeleton with fluttering rags; and as it came it cried three times, hoarsely: "Merritt, Merritt, Merritt!" and stumbled on past Merritt, looking neither to the right nor left, reeling drunkenly, panting like an overridden horse. An instant Merritt stood motionless with his men; but with the voice, he understood and leaped forward and caught the flying figure by its arm.

"Deane! *Deane!* For God's sake, what's happened?"

And Deane stumbled, recovered himself, reeled, and came slowly to the ground, with Merritt's arm about his shoulders, and his face hidden in his hands.

Merritt looked up, white to the lips with sheer fright.

"Get water, somebody!" he cried.

They brought him a cup, but Deane made no motion to take it until Merritt held it carefully to his lips. Then he snatched it, with a snarl like a hungry beast, and drained it and laughed hoarsely.

"Give me more!" he panted, and struggled to rise.

"There, old boy! keep cool!" Merritt soothed, and held him down. "Take it easy; you'll have enough."

He gave Deane the cup again, and splashed water on the grimed parched skin that drank as a plant drinks rain.

"I had bad times out there," Deane said suddenly. He spoke thickly, out of a stiff throat, with a curious eagerness, yet a certain hesitancy, in short, detached sentences. "My men deserted when I insisted on searching farther. They took all the food. And the water. You see"—the words came painfully—"I...didn't find him. Two nights ago—when was it? I forget. I've been out there years and years. But something happened. I saw something running away from me. So I chased it. And when I found it..." He broke off. "I don't know what I'm talking about. That morning I had been just within sight of your flag, so I was pretty sure of my direction. But I went on, keeping it as well as I could. I was nearly gone then. I heard your voices. And I ran, and called for you." Again he stopped.

Merritt, giving him drink, said uncertainly:

"I don't think I understand. Why do you say 'heard your voices'? Of course, you must have seen the camp before you heard us, or were we making such a racket——"

And after his words there came a pause, unexpected, pregnant with hidden meaning. Merritt suddenly saw Deane's hands slowly clench, with a strength which left the knuckles white, clench until they shook to the muscular effort. Deane said, very slowly, in a perfectly expressionless voice:

"I—thought you had found it out by this time. Merritt...I'm blind."

Again there was a pause. The cup in Merritt's hand remained tilted, its contents spilling upon the ground. Then he said, almost below his breath:

"How did it happen?"

"I'll tell you. Later. Can't we get inside somewhere? I feel the sun," Deane said. He got himself to his feet, unsteady, making a strong effort to get control of his weakness. Merritt passed an arm through his, and led him to his tent. A crowd of natives followed, curious as children, understanding nothing of what had passed....

That night, lying on his bed with a wet cloth about his head, Deane told his story to Merritt, in the darkness.

CHAPTER VII
THE OTHER WHO RETURNED

Merritt sat at the tent door, smoking, glancing now at the long figure on the bed, now out across the night to where the mounds loomed through the darkness. Deane's voice was low, and slow; at times he paused for minutes as though to gather fresh strength.

"I don't remember very clearly about parts of it," he said. "So if I get disconnected now and then, you'll know it's because I can't fit it all together. We searched in circles. For three days the men were all right. Then we worked around to the Rocks, where I had half expected to find at least the remains of the Arabs, but there was nothing. After we left the Rocks the men began to get ugly. They declared there was no use in looking further, and they wanted to return. Every day brought emptiness and failure. Holloway would not have been alive if we had found him, and although I hated to give up, I felt I could not risk the men's lives. So I said that the next day we'd start back. But that night a caravan passed us, twelve or fourteen miles away. My men deserted and went to join it. They took everything but my glass, my compass and waterskin, and what food I had with me. I started back.... I started back. On the"— he paused, with a visible effort to fix his attention on his words—"I think it was the third day, the water gave out. The next day at sunrise I saw the flag. It could not be seen with the naked eye; with the glass it was just

visible. If it had not been for that, I should have died—
out there. I covered a good many miles that morning.
There was not a scrap of shade, and the sun was cruel.
About noon I saw something running ahead. I thought
at first it might be Holloway, still alive by a miracle,
gone crazy, you know, with the sun. Anyhow, I was not
going to take chances. I chased it. Luckily for me, it
went in the general direction of the flag, due east. Then
I realised what I was doing, with the sun scorching like
a blast of furnace heat. But by that time the mischief
was done. My brain was burnt out; there was an iron
band across my forehead. I nearly went mad with the
pain. I think I got delirious after a while, for every time I
woke, I was chasing that infernal thing across the
desert. It stopped after a while. I thought it lay down,
but that may have been my eyes. I was seeing stars and
pinwheels then. And then something cracked inside my
head, and the light went out."

He drew a long breath. Always his voice was slow
and monotonous, devoid of all expression.

"For a while I...I stayed where I was. Then I swore
I'd get back in spite of it, or die on my feet. So I went on,
as nearly due east as I could guess, trying to keep in the
direction I had been started in. The fear that all
unconsciously I would get to walking in a circle, and so
keep on until my strength gave out; the feeling of
appalling helplessness, of not knowing whether I was
headed right or whether I might as well sit down where I
was and wait for the finish.... I tell you, Merritt, it was a
journey to Hell and back again." His voice shook, ever
so slightly. Merritt, in the doorway, turned his head
away.

"What I'm about to tell you now you may say is
nothing but the recollection of a delirium," the
monotonous, controlled voice went on. "I don't know
how long I had been travelling. It was slow work, as you

may guess. Suddenly I tripped over something. I felt around on the ground and my hands struck what had thrown me. It...it was a body, Merritt, a dried husk that sounded hollow when I struck it. I don't know whose. It might have been the boy's. They do dry up so fast, out in this sun, you know.... It was a shock, an awful one. I don't know what I did. I was so set, heart and soul, on keeping a straight course, that I scarcely dared turn my face aside or stop moving.... I felt for it, to see if I could tell anything by the clothes, but it slipped out of my hands and—and I could not find it again. I groped for it, but dared not move far to either side, lest I get turned around. It may have been lying within a foot of me, and I missed it. So I said—'God have mercy on your soul, whoever you were!' and went on, and left it lying there. But if it were Holloway—if it were the boy! To come across him, and not know him, and leave him!"—A sob shook him from head to foot. He continued, quietly as always.

"He's one of Us, of our speech and of our blood. And we were all he had out here.... It isn't profitable talking about those days that followed. I think there were three of them. My waterskin was empty; I chewed on dry biscuit until my mouth bled. In the mornings I set my course by the heat of the rising sun on my face. I broke out the crystal of my watch that I might feel the hands and know when they pointed to noon and the sun would be behind me. I had to travel in the morning so that I might have the feel of the sun to go by, and at night I was afraid to stir lest I get turned around. Oh, those nights! My God! those nights!" His voice dropped to a whisper. In a moment it went quietly on, restrained, devoid of all expression.

"Occasionally I had half-delirious dreams, which I could not distinctly remember afterwards. Usually I was in a garden, where the perfume of the jasmine and the honeysuckle was enough to drag the very heart out of you, and where a woman was with me, whose face I couldn't see. And I dreamt about the Princess a good deal—probably because I had had her on my mind—seeing her always as she must have been once, and never as the—the thing we found. In one dream, which I can remember, and which I'll never be able to forget, I saw the boy—our boy—in this garden place. He was lying face downward on the ground—I swear I could almost have touched him, it was so real! —and a woman was stooping over him—oh, Merritt, the loveliest thing that God or the Devil ever made! I never was much given to running after women, but—in that dream I wanted to strangle him, to crush the life and breath and soul out of him, because that woman was leaning over him, with her breath on him and her hands on his head, and *I* was mad for her. In a way, I could see myself creeping through that garden towards them, quite without volition of my own, parting the vines and the flowers carefully that they might not rustle. And as I got to them—" Deane stopped abruptly. His hand closed hard upon a corner of the blanket.

"As I got to them, the woman looked over her shoulder at me. From that point it's all confused and vague, as dreams will be, and I've lost the details. I only know that she left the boy lying on the ground, and moved away; that I followed her, and caught her, and she did not struggle, but put her arms about my neck and held her lips to mine. I tell you, I felt the weight of her body and the warmth of her breath as though I had held her in the flesh. And when earth and hell and heaven itself held nothing but the madness of her beauty, I felt a change. She seemed to stiffen in my grasp; her arms dropped from my shoulders. And then I saw a change. Saw it as plainly as though I had been awake and she was there in actual fact. I saw her flesh shrivel and the skin cling tight to the bones. I saw her face sink in until the eyes were gone, and the cheeks were gaunt and covered with wrinkled brown parchment, and the lips were grinning like the jaws of a skull. And the thing slid out of my arms and lay on the ground, stark and rigid. Then I thought that Holloway, from the ground, spoke, without moving, and said—'It isn't worth while, after all, is it?' And I woke in a cold sweat of abject terror, with his voice ringing in my ears so that I could have sworn that someone had just spoken.... Oh, it was maudlin, I don't deny it, and I was well over the edge of madness!" His voice all at once was strained and tired. "Three times I had that dream. I used to wait for it, and long for it, to intoxicate myself with her loveliness, but even in my sleep I was conscious of trying desperately to waken before the—the change should come. I never succeeded, and when I did wake, it was always in the same shiver of mortal fear, with that thing, dark and stiff, on the ground at my feet. And the third time..."

Again he stopped, controlling himself with an effort, gathering fresh strength to continue.

"Have you ever roused suddenly from sleep at night, for no apparent cause, and realised that your mind, your consciousness, was broadly awake while for a bare instant your body still slept, as it were? It gives you the physical sensation of sleep; you feel that your whole being is at lowest ebb, that your heart is beating slower, that your limbs are weighed down by faint numbness, that you are profoundly immovable. You are not, of course; when you make the conscious effort, you can move with perfect ease. It lasts barely a second. That is how I woke, the third time. And in that instant, while I lay feeling as though I could not stir hand or foot to save my soul, yet with every mental faculty waking to alertness, I got the impression of arms—soft human arms—removed from my neck, and knew that something beside me had sprung away, swiftly and silently. Dear Lord in heaven, how I cursed my blindness then! Not to know whether I was the plaything of strange forces, none the less real because I could not understand them, or whether it was all the workings of a fever-haunted brain—whether something was actually happening out there in the desert, or whether I was merely playing the fool—luckily with nobody at hand to take in the full beauty of the spectacle.... Oh, well! The only conclusion I can come to is that during those three days I was undoubtedly insane. And...I hope to God it's the correct one.... It seemed as though this went on for cycles of time; shivering nights spent half in a state of maudlin, sensuous bliss—half in a panic of crazy fear; blistering days, crawling on, inch by inch, over red-hot sands, in a blackness that was swimming with blood-red mist.... I soberly thought I had walked for weeks when I heard voices that sounded quite close at hand. I forgot that sound carries over the desert almost as over water, and thought I was right among you. I heard Ibraheem screaming to his 'Lord-God' about something, and I ran.... That's all."

His slow voice stopped with a gasp of utter exhaustion. And for a long space was silence.

When at last Merritt spoke, huskily, no answer came. He went to the bed, shielding his light with care, and stood looking down. Deane's gaunt frame was relaxed, his drawn face, graven into new deep lines of suffering, was quiet, his darkened eyes were closed. Merritt turned the lamp out and stole noiselessly from the tent....

In spite of Merritt's anxious care, Deane did not seem to rally from the effects of that desert journey. So that

Merritt wished to hasten the work, and get away, but to this Deane obstinately refused to listen. He argued forcefully that no time was like the present; that they did not know if they could ever get out again; that if his eyes could be cured at all, a few weeks' delay would not harm them. In the end Merritt yielded, partly because he wished to believe what Deane said, partly because all his heart was in his work. Soon Deane learned to go about by himself, with the aid of a stick, stumbling at first, for the ground was badly cut up, later with comparative ease and rapidity. That his helplessness was worse to him than the bitterness of death, Merritt knew unerringly. Of this Deane never spoke, but his face, when he failed in some erstwhile easy task, all unconsciously betrayed him. Continually he was restless, ill at ease, yet striving doggedly to get himself in hand. Merritt began to notice in him a desire for companionship, especially towards nightfall; noticed with opened eyes that Deane kept himself always near a group of men, even though he sat silent, taking no part in their talk. Twice, Merritt, going late at night cautiously to his tent to see that he wanted nothing, found it empty. At first this frightened him, suggesting thoughts of Deane wandering alone in the darkness, until he remembered that night and day were as the same to Deane.

So a week went by; and the Evil that brooded over them awoke once more and stalked abroad.

CHAPTER VIII
AT THE ELEVENTH HOUR

Merritt, in his tent, was busily bringing his journal down to date. The lamplight fell unsparingly on his grey face, weatherworn and with tired eyes, and flung a distorted shadow of him on the tent wall behind him. He wrote slowly, making no corrections, methodical, thorough, as in all his doings. The journal was a marvel of brevity and conciseness. His pen was finishing the sentence— "which I wish to present to the National Museum, in Washington, D. C, with the hope that my good friend, Dr. Peabody, may, on examination, be enabled to analyse what it contains." For it was of the lamp he wrote, the lamp, which, cold and dead, later found its place in a glass case among old relics of bygone days, labelled with a card bearing an outline of its half-known strange history, of which the beginning was forever lost. He was deep in interested review of its discovery, when a stumble at the door and a smothered curse announced the advent of Deane.

"Can I come in?" Deane asked, and entered hastily. He listened an instant to make sure of Merritt's position, and crossed the tent to him, feeling his way with the helpless awkwardness of the newly blind.

"Is there a piece torn out of the left sleeve of my shirt, near the shoulder?" he asked abruptly, and bent down that Merritt might observe. Merritt noticed that his breath was quick and his manner full of a repressed excitement.

"No," Merritt said. "Nothing wrong here."

"Thank the Lord for that," Deane muttered devoutly. "But then it's mighty queer. I don't understand what could have happened... Something caught at me just now, down in the diggings...I can't believe it's all imagination—"

Simultaneously Merritt exclaimed:

"Hold on! You said the left sleeve.

There's a six-inch rip in the right sleeve, here, where I'm pulling. Did you catch it on a nail?"

Deane drew his breath in sharply.

"There—is one, then?" he said in an odd voice. "No, I did not catch it on any nail."

Merritt turned to look at him.

"What's up?" he demanded.

But Deane, without noticing his question, began to speak rapidly, in the same tense voice.

"Then I believe anything—everything. I believe that the men are right. I believe the place is cursed. I believe that Bob and the Arabs were decoyed and trapped by unhuman powers. I've scoffed and sneered, but now I will believe anything this land can show me. I'm beaten—done up. I don't understand but I believe.... I believe it!"

His voice dropped to a hoarse whisper. Merritt stood up and shook him gently.

"Look here, old man, this won't do. Get yourself together. It won't last much longer; in ten days at most we'll be off."

"Ten days," Deane repeated. "Ten days.... I guess I can stand that, can't I?"

"If you think you'd like to start ahead of me," Merritt said, "take what stores and men you want, and start on first. I think that would be the best plan, anyhow. Your eyes need treatment; it may be a serious thing if they don't get it soon. I won't be long behind you—"

But Deane interrupted with sudden fierceness, a burst of uncalled-for anger, so that Merritt stared at him in sheer amazement.

"See here! Don't say that to me again; understand? Why, do you know what you're inviting me to do? Play the coward—run away and hide my head in the sand; make a worse spectacle of myself than I am already. That's what you're asking me to do! But I won't—by Heaven, I won't! Don't think that because I'm useless and not worth my salt I'll let a man—any man—insult me——"

But, on the word, his voice changed and hesitated; his torrent of speech checked. He said with a certain timidity which sat very strangely on him—a deprecating humility not good to hear:

"I—I don't mean that, Merritt, upon my soul, I don't! I don't know what I'm talking about, these days."

"You go to bed," Merritt said with decision. "That's the best place for you at present. Sleeping pretty good, lately?"

"Not ten minutes since—since I got back," Deane answered shortly. "Sometimes I get half off, but that—that's worse than nothing. Every time I drop off I'm back—out there—again, stumbling over rocks, mad with hunger and thirst." He brushed the back of a hand across his forehead. "Or else I'm feeling dry arms around my neck, and something pulling at me the way—oh, the way I dreamt out there!" He shuddered. "Then I stay awake the rest of the night."

"Deane, go home!" Merritt urged earnestly. "You're not fit to stay out here. No man would be, after—all that."

But on the instant Deane's anger flared up again, irresponsible, violent, wholly out of proportion to its cause.

"Haven't I got enough to keep me happy without you to help it on?" he said with savage irony. "Do you think I'll turn tail and give up now, at the eleventh hour?"

"No; after all I suppose it would not do," Merritt said gravely, a keen eye on Deane's drawn face.

Deane calmed down at once.

"I thought you'd feel that way about it," he said in satisfied tones. "You see, of course, how I'm placed." He laughed grimly, jangling laughter that jarred. "Lord, what a farce it is! Here I'm going the way Holloway went; coming to you whining to be put to sleep, as he came to me, poor devil! Next thing, I'll be crawling around your tent to hear you moving inside; then I'll be wandering down among the tombs; then——"

"Now what are you talking about?" Merritt demanded helplessly. "Don't think about Holloway any more, there's a good chap. Suppose I fix you up something to take, and you turn in——"

"The devil you will!" Deane retorted with promptness. "You don't get around me that way, by George! I've fixed up stuff for shaky devils myself before this, and sent 'em to sleep thinking they had a good strong dose inside them. None of your lime-juice-and-water tricks for me!"

Merritt gasped slightly.

"Oh—very well. Then I'll look in later to see how you are getting on."

He turned to his journal again. Deane, on his way to the door, said calmly over his shoulder:

"Then you'd better sing out loud before you come in. Hamd—that black limb of Satan—came in on me suddenly last night, and I choked him silly before he could tell me who he was. I haven't got a rag of nerve left, that's the truth of it."

He departed, swearing a little as he ran against a camp-stool in his path.

"Yes sir! he's reached his limit. I've got to get him out of this somehow," said Merritt, and took up his pen once more.

But later, when Merritt, loudly heralding his approach, entered Deane's tent, Deane was not within. Merritt stood in the doorway and looked about him, scowling uneasily.

"Wish I'd kept him with me," he said aloud. "The fellow isn't fit to be left alone just now. He might—good Lord! why, he might...."

He sat down on the leather-covered trunk and waited. Outside, the night was very still. No sound came from the camps; all the world slept. Merritt dozed uncomfortably, his head fallen forward, hands hanging limp between his knees. It seemed to him, afterwards, that he had slept thus a very long time. As one, in ten minutes, may dream through a cycle of time, so Merritt felt as though half the night had gone when at length he pulled himself together, guiltily conscious that he ought to go and look for Deane. He yawned, stretched, and got himself to his feet, stupid with sleep, noticing, irrelevantly, that the lamp was still burning, and that the moonlight, coming through the open entrance, turned its light wan and sickly. And then he started, wide awake on the instant, listening with bent head and hands clenching to a sound that came out of the night; a moan, rising and swelling into a scream that split through the stillness, and stopped suddenly as though choked into strangled quiet, with the silence settling deeper than before. The cry came from the excavations. Merritt dashed out of the tent and ran thither, his teeth set hard, every muscle tense to face he knew not what crisis. But that some crisis was at hand, instinct told him surely.

He gained the edge of the level which overlooked the courtyard, forty feet below, and looked down. There, among the exhumed tombs, was dense black shadow, save at one place only, in the centre of the open court, where the moonlight fell like a lake of silver at the bottom of a well. Merritt, pausing uncertain which way to turn or what to look for, heard strange sounds arising from the heart of the shadow below him; heavy breathing, guttural snarls, low and worrying, like an angry dog's; thumping as of heavy bodies at grips and threshing to and fro. Then a thing appeared, from the blackness into the patch of light, and Merritt rubbed his eyes to make sure that the wan moonlight, which turned all things uncorporeal as phantoms, had not deceived him—a thing that rolled upon the ground, and rose and fell again in contorted struggling—an indeterminate mass, black against the silver, silent save for deep panting breaths and worrying snarls. Merritt plunged down the slanting gallery leading to the courtyard, leaping downward with great strides. Even as he raced, his brain formulated theories. It might be a wild animal—lion—hyena—jackal; it might be a native run amuck; it might be a thief. Whatever it was, it had Deane, handicapped by his blindness and recent hardships, down and fighting for his life——

Merritt gained the lower level, stumbled over an unseen obstruction in his path, recovered, and dashed into the courtyard to where the struggling mass had been. Had been, but was no longer; for even in the bare half-minute that Merritt had taken in his descent, what was to happen had happened. There was only a crumpled heap upon the ground in the moonlight, that screamed when Merritt touched it, and clutched him, feeling with blind, desperate fingers for his throat. Merritt cried sharply:

"Stop it, Deane, stop it, I tell you! It's I, Merritt! Oh, man, are you off your head entirely?"

With difficulty he mastered him, and held him down, repeating over and over: "It's I—it's only Merritt. Don't fight like this, man—can't you understand—it's Merritt!"

Until Deane's struggles ceased, and he lay panting, with Merritt's weight atop of him.

"You—Merritt?" he said faintly. Merritt, still holding him, repeated soothing assurances automatically. But Deane sat up suddenly, flinging off Merritt as though he had been a child, and cried:

"Then where is it? Merritt, Merritt, find it—find it for the love of Heaven, and burn it! It can't have got very far—I had it sure. Oh, go, old man, look for it—it's here among the tombs somewhere! I had it not half a minute ago!"

Merritt put a hand on his arm, and felt that he was shaking all over.

"Steady, old boy!" he said. "Get yourself together. There's nothing here—I'll swear there isn't. What was it you were doing?"

"Doing!" Deane said between his teeth. His hands clenched and unclenched convulsively. "I tell you I had it! Can't you do as I tell you? Do you want the thing to get away from us again? Oh, man, do as I tell you!"

"Hold on a minute! What was it you had?" Merritt asked. Deane's voice rose to a shriek of angry impotence.

"The mummy, you fool, the mummy! Can't you understand? Will you look for it, damn you!"

"The mummy!" Merritt echoed blankly. The solution of Deane's conduct flashed upon him; Deane was undoubtedly mad; the overwrought brain at last had given way. But Deane was speaking, in a high, shrill voice that staggered and stuttered crazily.

"I found it here, down among the tombs. I knew I should; I was waiting for it. It came, and I felt its arms around my neck, and I knew that the dream I had in the desert was no dream. And when I tried to get away, it clung, clung like a leech, with feet and hands and teeth—*Merritt!* Oh, my God, Merritt, where are you!" It was the voice of a child, wakened suddenly, in mortal terror to find itself in the dark.

Merritt, with instant comprehension, said quickly:

"Here, old chap! It's all right—I'm here. I won't go off."

Deane's hand groped for his, and clutched it with a grip which made Merritt wince. His voice took up its tale.

"I fought it off, and it twined its legs and arms around mine and I couldn't shake it off. I tried to beat its head on the stones, and it fastened its teeth in my shoulder and held on. Then I tried to bring it up above. I let it cling, and held on to it, and ran; but I had lost my bearings and went round and round without getting anywhere. I reached the gallery at last, but it found out what I was doing, and fought—God! how it fought to get away! I tripped it, and we both fell, it trying to break loose, and I trying to hold it down. And then I heard a shout, and steps coming, and it tore away from me, and I lost it."

"Well, come away!" Merritt said soothingly. To himself he said with sternness, "One of us jackasses has got to keep cool!"

Deane must be humoured; must be coaxed into submission. Deane laughed. "You think I'm mad, do you?" he cried. "Well, I'm not. Not yet. I'm—I'm as sane as you are, but I won't be very long. If you had felt it hanging to you, with its skinny arms wound round you, and you not able to see what it was—perhaps you'd be half-mad too."

"It couldn't have been the—the mummy, you know," Merritt said, as one trying to soothe a child to reason. "That's quite absurd. A mummy couldn't possibly be waltzing around like this. It's not in the nature of things——"

"Of course it's not in the nature of things!" Deane cut in savagely. "Don't I know that?" His voice wavered; became shriller. "I can't stand it any longer, Merritt. Call me any name you like—I deserve it. But I'm—I'm—" He laughed again, crazily, so that Merritt started apprehensively; and suddenly buried his face in his hands and sat with long shudders chasing through him. "I'm done up," he said hoarsely.

"Get up and come with me," Merritt ordered. He caught himself casting a wary eye around; Deane's collapse had unsteadied even his well-strung nerves. "We'll not stay here another day. This place is—is unholy, that's all there is to it. Come away, old man."

He got Deane to his feet, and Deane clung to him helplessly, begging not to be left alone. Carefully Merritt led him up to the slanting gallery, over the cut-up ground, and to his own tent. Here Deane sat obediently on the bed, turning his white, haunted face always towards the sound of Merritt's comings and goings about the tent. Merritt saw with a sense of shock that his shirt had been torn into ribbons on one side, and on his shoulder was blood and the mark of teeth. He washed the wound and touched it with lunar caustic; and Deane laughed grimly through locked jaws. Then Merritt put him to bed, and lay down himself where Deane might touch him and be instantly convinced of his presence, leaving the lamp still burning.

The tent fell into silence; but Merritt, always wakeful, with every nerve strung taut, felt subtly the tenseness of the figure beside him; knew how Deane, motionless, was holding himself down by sheer force of will; and longed feverishly for daylight when the nightmare of the darkness should end. Once, indeed, he dozed uneasily, only to be wakened by Deane's hands, wet with sweat, playing over his face, and Deane's voice whispering:

"It's out there. I hear it. Merritt, if it comes in here I shall go mad!"

And Merritt, startled into quick consciousness, sprang up and peered through the tent-flap into the night, before he realised the foolishness of his action, and the credulity it implied.

"See it?" Deane asked tensely behind him. "If it's there, I'm going out after it. I can't stand the notion of its going around loose any longer. Suppose it came in here..."

And Merritt paused a perceptible instant before replying. Then he said:

"Nothing out there——"

And came back and lay down again. But he did not tell Deane that something had slipped out of his sight, behind a mound into the shadows not a dozen yards away; something, if his eyes did not deceive him, which was not a goat at large, nor a hyena, nor any creature that walked upon four legs. And there was no noise in the camps to indicate that men were stirring there.

Once more there fell a silence. Out of it Deane suddenly spoke again, with a jarring laugh.

"This is a hell of a place, isn't it?" And then, "Oh, boy, boy! If we hadn't scoffed and been quite so confoundedly cocksure of ourselves and our theories!"

Morning broke. Before the sky had wholly lost its veil of night, Merritt called Ibraheem. He came; but if he drew conclusions from the two grey and drawn faces before him, he made no sign. To him Merritt gave certain orders; he ejaculated in profane and joyful English and departed. Fifteen minutes later the camps were all astir. Breakfast was being cooked and eaten, as before, but there was an added hum of preparation and anticipation. The cases containing tablets and antiquities were loaded carefully on camels; the camp dunnage was collected and packed; at noon the tents were struck. All hands helped; four were eagerly ready to do the work of one. The East had conquered; whatever means she had employed to hide the remainder of her treasures from the eyes of the prying West, had done their work. The grave, half-opened, was to be left in peace. Her methods, lawful or unlawful, had sufficed.

At sunset the caravan started. Merritt, his grey face and tired eyes seemingly unchanged, sober, yet with the activity of one who, in authority, must be all things to all men, urged on the advance. Deane, silent, with brooding face and bowed shoulders, sat his horse listlessly, leaving its control to the Arab who held the leading-rein. His reddish hair was touched with grey; the lines of humour about his mouth had given place to other lines, which cast the face into a new mould; he looked aged by many years. The sun, shooting his last level rays across the desert, fell full upon their faces as they set out upon their journey, leaving their work half-done.

The vanguard drew away over the desert, a long string of horses and men and camels. In the last moment of twilight, when the sky was steeped in violet, and the darkness rushed down upon them with swooping wings, Merritt turned in his saddle and looked back at the scene of his work. The excavations, only hastily filled up, gaped like open wounds—wounds which might never heal, but remain always open to the pitiless sun and the driving sand-storms and the holy nights—half-revealing, half-concealing the secrets which lay below. The half-buried corpse of the city that had been, sank again to its broken rest, to lie a while in pitiful nakedness, and be slowly buried once more, in the fulness of time, beneath the shifting sand. Man had come, and man had gone; man had come again, and now had gone, and the earth would reclaim her own. The inscrutable East, brooding and sombre, wise with forgotten evil lore, had conquered.

A sick goat, left behind as worthless, ran a few steps after the caravan, bleating feebly. It stopped in front of one of the mounds, and looked after them, as horses and men moved slowly across the desert. Occasionally, from in front, voices were heard, growing always fainter as the dark string wound its way westward against the stars. But those in the rear were very silent. Merritt, looking back, saw something slipping among the mounds, a black blot against the dusk, and struck the spurs into his horse's flank. Then he remembered that it might have been the goat.

Then the curtain of night shut down, and the stealthy moving thing was blotted from his sight.

Other books from Dead Letter Press:

THE MYSTERIOUS FLAME *by Orrin Grey* **OUT OF PRINT**
(Limited-edition softcover chapbook, January 2009)

ENGELBRECHT AGAIN! *by Rhys Hughes*
(Limited-edition hardcover, October 2008)

THE KING OF DEADTOWN *by Glynn Barrass* **OUT OF PRINT**
(Limited-edition softcover chapbook, March 2008)

BOUND FOR EVIL: CURIOUS TALES OF BOOKS GONE BAD
edited by Tom English (Limited-edition hardcover, January 2008)
OUT OF PRINT

PHANTASMAPEDIA *by Mark McLaughlin* **OUT OF PRINT**
(Limited-edition softcover chapbook, November 2007)

BLOOD COVEN *by Christopher Fulbright & Angeline Hawkes*
(Limited-edition softcover chapbook, May 2007) **OUT OF PRINT**

DEAD LETTER PRESS
BOX 134 NEW KENT, VA 23124-0134
WWW.DEADLETTERPRESS.COM

THE LITERARY VAMPIRE SERIES *edited by Tom English*
(These are the titles of the original series, issued as limited-edition
softcover chapbooks, May 2005-2010) **ALL ARE OUT OF PRINT.**